THE CORDS OF
ORION

Book One *The*
Dominant
Arise

Gary Henderson

ISBN 978-1-937975-04-3
First edition, paperback format

Electronic books available as ISBN 978-1-937975-05-0

RNWC Media, LLC
PO Box 559
Pinehurst, TX 77362

www.RNWCMedia.com

www.OrionTheBook.com
www.TheCordsOfOrion.com
www.TheDominantArise.com

Prologue

A scream and metallic crash jerked my attention to the front of the plane. I leaned over, straining to look down the aisle, and lots of other people did too. A bald man in a black coat and faded jeans was hacking at the door into the cockpit. I could see bare legs, I guess one of the stewardesses, lying on the floor behind him. He kept kicking back at her body, as though it were in his way.

The pilot came on the intercom. Sounded like a young guy, scared. He said, "Get in your seats. Brace for impact!" The nose of the plane suddenly dropped, and we were falling out of the sky. The people who were out of their seats never had a chance to get back into them.

We went straight down, best I could tell, from thirty thousand feet. The guy hammering on the door fell, then stood up on the door, which was now below him, and began shooting into it. I don't know where the gun came from, but he had one. I guess he killed the pilots. He never got that door open. The plane began tumbling; I lost all sense of up or down. I squeezed the armrests, tried to focus on the seat in front of me, and just endured the horrible sensation, trying not to throw up. Books and cups and laptops flew through the air. Panicked screams and prayers filled the plane. It seemed to last forever, and then we slammed into the ground.

The world exploded. The plane crumpled in, a tin can suddenly smashed from all sides, and we were inside. Everything crushed against everything else. In the midst of chaos and sudden agony and the inferno of exploding jet fuel, blackness swallowed me up.

A moment passed, surely no more. I opened my eyes. All the pain was gone. The horrific fire and smoke swirled around us, but left us untouched. All around me, others straightened up and looked at each other. Some hugged those next to them. We stared at each other in amazement.

I don't think anyone lived through it. We slowly moved away from the wreckage and fire, because our bodies were destroyed, of course. One little child was still clinging to his body. There was not enough left of it for him to live in it again, and I helped him let go. A violent explosion consumed what was left of the plane. Nothing remained. I remember cars, and a truck or two, so maybe there was a road and some traffic there.

As we wandered away from the wreckage and out into a pasture, grazing cows stared at us from higher ground in the distance. Or at the fire, really, I doubt they saw us.

I noticed a man walking among the people, a head taller than anyone else, and as bright as the fire we had just left. He spoke to each one, and touched them, carefully and only once, as though he were conveying something specific. He wore a simple robe, and a quiet, almost hidden power was in him. A power you could trust, I thought, not a power to fear.

He looked at me, with eyes as deep blue as the evening sky just before the stars leap out, and a smile that would not be refused. His hand paused just before it reached me, as though it were only an offer, not yet quite given, a gift that needed acceptance. I found myself leaning into his touch, and in an instant peace flooded my heart. I relaxed and took a deep, deep breath.

He touched the last one standing there and turned toward the crowd that now was entirely focused on his face. He ignored the gathering cars, the fire engines, the billowing inferno, the sirens.

"Come."

Come?

A thousand questions threw themselves into my mind. Where? Come where? After all the talk about life after death, after years of wondering and study and speculation and argument and chosen belief, I found myself with no answers at all. What was about to happen? Where was he taking us? Who was he, really?

"Come," he said, and there was no doing otherwise. We came.

One

It was Thursday when I met Him.

Funny how time still goes on. I always thought of eternity as a time without ... well, time. But it makes sense. Planets still spin, tides still flow, seasons change. Years pass. It just doesn't matter in the way it used to. We're not being used up, like we were. We're actually... what? Strengthening? Becoming more real? I don't know, but I feel it, and I see it in the others. There's a real peace that comes from the knowledge that this never ends. There's no rush. No hurry. We've got time.

If that makes sense.

Of course, what day of the week it is... that's gone. Once that Thursday was past, it ceased to matter. For us, anyway. For me.

He was so matter-of-fact about my arrival, and seemed delighted, as though welcoming a long-awaited houseguest. Naturally, He had known forever that I would be there that day. And I had been more certain about Him, more settled, as the day approached. Though I didn't know, of course, at the time, that the day was actually approaching quite that soon. We always think we have years to go, I suppose. And then when it happens, you're so caught up in the event that there's no time to prepare for what comes next. Whatever preparation you've made, whatever relationship you're already walking in with Him, well, there you are.

And there I was.

He seemed to be waiting for me, with a small group gathered around. As I arrived, He looked at me, and the face I had so longed to see was suddenly before me. I could not speak. Suddenly everything was clear, everything was settled. I knew, and He knew, everything there was to know about my life, everything I had ever thought, felt, or done, and the only thing that mattered was what He had done for me. The rest was gone, and all was new. Completely new.

"Well done," He smiled, and I knew instantly every moment of my life He was blessing. Every time I followed His lead, yielded to His touch, and saw His power and healing flow into the world through my obedience. Gold and silver, precious jewels, never to be lost. All else was gone.

A sudden panic swept over me, swirling with remorse. What about my family? What about all that was left undone, all those people and things that had consumed my attention on earth, just … just moments ago?

He must have known my mind even as the thoughts arose, and with His look a confident peace rose in my heart, a certain knowledge that His hands held them all. The panic seeped away. Peace beyond understanding. His peace.

They welcomed me into the group. Clearly they had all known I was coming. Who were these people?

Linus towered over me, and his bear hug enveloped me in strength and in the smell of woven linen. Julia's red hair blazed in the morning sun, and her smile was all freckles and impish mischief, forecasting an eternity of unpredictable moments!

The morning sun?

John's serious blue eyes caught mine, and pressed in to know what sort of man was joining their company. In a moment I knew him, and I suppose he knew me. Knowing, as we were known; He said it would be like this!

Where *was* that light coming from? There was no morning sun. How could there be? There was no "morning" anymore!

It flowed from nowhere and everywhere, delighting itself in eluding the eye and playing upon whatever you looked upon to present that thing, to your eye, in that moment, in the most glorious light possible. Beauty was everywhere, and I realized it was continually being put on display by the living light, moving and changing and leading the eye to new delights in every direction.

He was watching me and laughed as I realized it. Enjoying the effects of His creation on those He created it for, I suppose! I laughed as well, a joy flowing up within me that seemed to complete the healing of all that had come before. I was home...

Home.

I needed some time to be alone, to say my own goodbyes to those I had left so suddenly. The sweet face of my life-long love filled my mind. I would never touch the curve of her cheek again, after so many years together. I could see her tears as though I were there, and I ached to hold her. And my little ones – not so little any more, really. I saw them come close around her. They'll watch over my love, and the new babies they bring will give her comfort.

I left the group to wander and stare at the beauty around us. I looked quickly for my camera, and had to laugh at myself. Who needs a camera in heaven? I wandered out the main gates and down a winding road, through meadows dancing with color, to a bank of clouds that came up to the road like fog on a high mountain pass. I stepped out onto the clouds and began running, just with the delight of being there and being able to do it.

I wished for a sunset and the ability to run in the clouds before it.

I came to a towering mountain of cumulus clouds blazing white on one side, facing the late afternoon sun, with feathered plains flowing away from the feet of the mountain. Behind it deeply shadowed flanks accented the stark white tumbling mass.

The clouds in front of me seemed pure mist, soft and featureless. But there it was, the sun, setting in front of me to the left, casting a soft orange glow over all the landscape before me.

If the sun were setting, and these were clouds, I must be above the earth. How had I gotten there? I looked behind me and saw no road, no meadow, no gates, just more blue sky and higher clouds bathed in the same glow of the evening light.

Ahead, the misty landscape was broken by low cumulus clouds, foothills rising up in clusters. Their rims glowed with backlit edges, and the color washed from bright orange down to deep purple at the bottom.

Rows of tumbled ridges followed one after another then faded back into the mist. An island of ruffled hills drifted in the sea of softness.

Further ahead a massive thunderhead rose up, blue and purple and dark grey, an ethereal mountain casting dark shadows across the cloudy plains. It rose thousands of feet through another layer of orange, purple, and white cloud above me, then spread out into a flat-iron crest, deep blue-grey on the side towards me, pure white at the top where the sun smote it fully, and glowing orange around the edges all the way down. A cloud of rain drifted down the north side, diffusing a grey screen across the orange of the more distant clouds. A cirrus horsetail drifted up in front of it, delicate wisps of orange against the soft grey behind them.

In moments I was sitting on the mountain's crest and staring into the heart of old Sol, a magnificent sight my earthly eyes could never have taken in. The deeper I looked, the more intently I focused, the more I could see of the nuclear holocaust, until I was watching the liquid fire swirl and explode at its very core.

Then I ran straight down the tumbling masses and across the flowing plain, with no sense of tiring or fear or being lost, though I had no idea where I really was, if 'where' even mattered.

On an impulse I dove into the mist at my feet. It offered no resistance. Passing through a deep layer of grey below the orange-washed surface, I came out into evening dusk with a landscape below of farmland, roads, and a great river weaving its way through the greens and browns. Miles ahead of me the river, splattered with white and deeply shadowed by cliffs rising on either side, suddenly dropped out of sight.

I flew towards the cliffs, still diving from where I had been, moving effortlessly through occasional drifting clouds, one layer below the next. The sun broke through underneath the clouds above me and painted the land below with a brilliant backlighting, a deep red glow playing on the horizon. Glancing behind me, I saw no shadow on the clouds where mine should have been. A softly glowing rainbow formed a full circle around the spot.

Coming to the river, I drifted in between the shadowed cliffs. The evening light touched the top of the eastern cliffs, but night was falling quickly. I stepped onto one of the boulders in the middle of the stream, and the river threw white water high in the air all around me as it crashed into the stone. Lifting my hands to heaven, I whispered, "Thank you, Father, for all this beauty, and for eternity to enjoy it."

The roar of a waterfall called to me from just ahead. Somehow knowing I had nothing to fear, I dropped into the water rushing and crashing about my feet. I landed on the gravel bottom of the stream, with waters streaming and surging past, but pushing me not at all. A big trout hung in the backwash behind the boulder I had stood on, not startled at all by my sudden arrival.

"Of course not," I said. "He can't see me."

Did I just speak? Underwater? Apparently! I laughed, then marveled at that as well.

Pushing off from the streambed, I floated just above it, deep within the river, and swam around the rocks as they emerged. Suddenly the floor of the stream changed from gravel to rock, and the water seemed to speed up. I braced myself, and as the riverbed dropped suddenly away, the water about me plunged down with it. I floated straight out over the falling, crashing water and the clouds of mist and spray boiling up from the bottom of the falls.

Far below me the stream now swirled and bubbled, smoothing itself out into a new path soon bordered by pastures and fenced farmlands. Night covered the land as I drifted above it, and lights came on in the homes and barns.

I decided to return to the sky, and the very thought became action; the land and river dropped away into the distance below me.

As I reached the first layer of clouds, all was dark below me, out to the horizon where a narrow band of deep red spanned the edge of the world, diffusing quickly into a sky of orange and pale blue. A thin band of cloud spanned the horizon above it, offering a stripe of deep grey with feather-tips of bright orange on the bottom side where the sun, almost below the horizon, still reached that band for a few more minutes. Suddenly the tips of orange gave way to fiery red; a bare sliver of the sun threw a final splash of color on it before disappearing.

I paused to watch the transition. In moments the sun was gone. The flame red died to an ashen grey, with the pale blue of the sky above quickly fading to deeper blue, purple, then black. Stars sprang out to decorate the velvet deep.

Behind me the moon was rising, full and bright. I turned toward it, and willed myself to a great speed, crossing the distance more quickly than I could have imagined possible. I knew something of the physical distance involved, and it crossed my mind that such things simply did not matter anymore.

The face of the moon was in full daylight, but my eyes made the adjustment naturally and easily from the total blackness behind it to the overwhelming brightness of the sun reflecting off the dust. Almost immediately I stood on the surface of the moon, my feet sinking an inch or two into a powdery softness.

I sensed the Spirit with me as I stood looking at the Earth, backlit below the Sun. He seemed to be enjoying the beauty of it as much as I was, and I delighted in His presence. "Thank you," I whispered again.

When I had gazed for a time, I was ready to return Home. Not knowing quite how to do it, I simply turned my mind to the Gates I had left, and willed to move in that direction. The scene behind me disappeared, and the road up to the Gates was under my feet. I strolled along enjoying the fragrance of the wide, flowered pastures and the fruit trees that lined the way, until I passed into the Gates once again and on to the home … and the adventure … he had prepared for me.

Job and Jolina sat in a side room on the first floor of the four-story mansion, sipping lemonade. She thought back over their long life together.

"It was devastating when everything came apart." She looked at him, before continuing. "You were amazing. I gave up long before the end, as you know, and I'm sorry. You were right to pursue Him, to believe in His love in spite of all the pain."

Job smiled at the one who had borne all his children. "You are so beautiful."

She laughed. "You always thought so!"

"And He healed our sorrows afterward, and now has healed them forever. What more could we ask?"

"Nothing, nothing at all," she agreed. "But now your new adventure begins."

"With some interesting companions."

"You haven't said much about what you expect. Has He told you?"

Job pulled another of his favorite apples from the bowl between them, and bit slowly into it. Jolina studied the man. His peace and confident strength were still a delight to her.

"These are really good," he said, when his mouth wasn't so full.

She waited.

"We have a new role to play." He looked intently at her, and a smile slowly spread across his face. "Like what Adam did. But more, much more!"

She strained to keep from laughing at the little boy she saw within him, the child's excitement at a new adventure. She gave up, and laughed.

"What?" A hurt look replaced his secretive smile.

"I'm sorry," she managed to say, wiping her eyes. "I'm sorry. Go on. Your new role?"

"He's sending us to new worlds. Think of it! New, completely new, and waiting for us!"

She searched his eyes, wondering at the immensity of God's intent.

"Like Adam," he continued, "but more. More than Adam. He was the gardener, as Father created the garden, created Eden, and populated the Earth. But now ..."

He shook his head.

"Now our word -- God's word, in our mouth -- carries power. We'll do as we always do, of course, watching and listening for Him, for His will, and then moving in that. But the balance has shifted; we have power now. As Jesus did! Much more than Adam ever knew."

She stared at him, trying to comprehend. To speak new life into being? To participate in creation itself, new creation? How would that ..?

Then something else occurred to her.

"Job, you've always had hundreds, or thousands, at your side. Now you go to danger, adventure, challenges we don't know, with … with four."

"Five."

She counted the ones she knew about. "Who else?"

"He said He would never leave us … I think that makes five!"

"Yes, of course, you're right," she laughed, and chose peace.

They sat quiet for a moment. "Is there more?"

He pursed his lips, and looked down.

"You know Leviathan was captive on Earth with the angels who rebelled…"

He looked up at her, and she nodded.

"But his kin were not. His spawn. Father scattered them across the stars. I don't know if they're all in rebellion, or how much they can do… but I think one of them is close to … is being held … where we'll be."

"Really! Of all the places in the universe … that's not accidental!"

"No, obviously not."

Imagining those creatures held in physical form was hard enough. Imagining their attitude, and what they might do … was even worse. She looked at him.

"He offers repentance to all," suggested Job, with a shrug. "Perhaps it is offered to them as well. Perhaps our task is to be there when this creature decides."

She nodded grimly. "Perhaps so."

She decided not to consider what might happen if that decision did not go well.

Two

He awoke hungry.

Rousing slowly, Livya-Gadol, son of Leviathan, uncurled his long body and looked about. The damp, murky cave was empty, and smelled of nothing in particular.

How long have I slept? Where has He put me?

Outside, the sky offered no particular help. Deep, deep black, with billions of stars, but no familiar patterns. No Pleiades, no Bear, no ... Orion.

He put me in Orion.

Memory flooded back.

Lucifer had recruited an army and challenged ... Him. Challenged God Himself.

What a fool, what a proud, beautiful fool. The masterpiece of Creation, but that wasn't enough. He had seen what was coming next, the crowning glory of God's masterwork, and was enraged at the idea. Furious that something else would be created, something in His image, that would take precedence even over Lucifer, over the most beautiful being ever to exist. The idea was intolerable to him.

So Lucifer gathered his forces, and they fought, and the Universe was blasted in the battle. Earth would be remade, and the Plan would proceed. God's plan, not Lucifer's.

Lucifer, and all the angels with him, had been thrown down to Earth and locked in.

But what about us? Leviathan's kin, the "sons of Pride", the Dominant. We were ... dispersed. Caged.

Not angels, but swept up in the rebellion with them. Not to be kept imprisoned on Earth, like them, but imprisoned nonetheless, given time to reflect.

We did not actually "leave our rightful places," so He gave us time to make a new choice.

Or not.

Hunger growled insistently. It was a new sensation to him, but unmistakable in its meaning. Looking around, the creature saw no shrubbery, no ferns, no trees. A pool, black in the starlight, offered refreshment and the hope of catching something edible. Surf pounded close by, just out of sight. Angry, violent surf.

At Home, eating was for pleasure. Clearly it was more than that in this place, and would be something crucial to existence. What an odd thought.

Are others here? Leviathan was thrown to Earth, with Lucifer. But the others? Am I alone somewhere in Orion?

Hunger was so foreign to his experience that it spawned a new thought.

I'm physical. How did that happen?

Feeling of his muscles, stretching, easing out to full length, he moved to the pool. Sliding into the water, he found it cool, and sweet to drink. And empty. Nothing lived there, to his surprise. But a current moved through it, from the desert towards the sound of the sea.

Two moons were rising. Under the pale light he saw gravel, and sand, and rocky mountains rising around him. No vegetation at all.

Truly a prison planet.

Suddenly very tired, he slithered back into the cave and curled up into dark and sour dreams.

"Are you ready?"

Jesus smiled, obviously knowing the answer. I had never been more ready in my life.

"Father asked Job if he could 'restrain the Pleiades' and 'loose the cords of Orion.' At the time, Job could not possibly have answered."

He looked around at us. "But now he has done so, and he is ready. Ready to 'loose the cords of Orion.' You'll join him to begin the task;

when Orion is free, others will pick up the work from there."

I was stunned. I knew the verse well -- it had always fired my imagination. What in the world -- what in the heavens? -- could it mean, to "loose the cords" of Orion?

"It always spoke to your heart because of the part you have to play," He explained, as my thoughts must have visibly run across my face. "Linus and Julia felt the same. You'll go together, and John will join you. Are you ready? Job is waiting."

Job was strolling in a courtyard garden of apple and pear trees, working on a red Perfect Delight that I could smell from 50 yards away. This was the apple that all those trees on Earth were trying to produce! My mouth watered, and I was soon sharing his pleasure with a crisp, juicy sample of my own.

Suddenly it was clear. So many things we knew on Earth were simply copies of the reality that awaited us, the reality that now surrounded us. Those were references to horses, and trees, and mountains, but with a nature much more responsive to Him than the ones we knew. Had we not realized what we were reading? And the temple, built exactly like the one in Heaven. Did we not understand? Copies on earth of the realities in the heavenlies, to encourage us, to help us believe, to help us understand what he was preparing for eternity. Including apples!

Job looked us over. He was a man used to command, used to leading groups and accomplishing whatever his hand found to do. His smile took us all in, and I thought he was comparing one or two of us with his own sons and daughters. I decided to ask one of those questions that had always puzzled me.

"Job, tell me something."

He lifted an eyebrow, and a smile began working its way across his mouth. I suddenly realized my question was probably nothing new. I forged ahead.

"God said you would have three times the sons and daughters you lost, but the scriptures only describe twice the number." He laughed, and waved a hand towards the mansion rising behind the courtyard, with many windows reflecting the golden sky. "They're all here! My first family, and my second! I have them all!"

Of course. One plus two makes three.

I blushed with the obvious answer. Would I find all the "hard questions" that troubled me on earth answered so readily?

Morning surprised him with its heat and oppressive light. Hunger raged in his belly. Almost without thinking, Livya-Gadol moved out of the cave and towards the sound of a great sea pounding its fists against a rocky coast. The cliff dropped away so suddenly he almost fell over it, down into the white foam of tall waves throwing themselves into a wall of rock that rose up from the surf below. Forgetting he was now held within a physical body, he leapt forward into the air, and found himself falling toward the wet rocks below. Instinct took over. His great wings unfolded, caught the air, and swept him up from the spray.

Of course. Of course I can fly. I've always had wings. Now they're ... physical.

He worked with them, learning to turn, to dive, to soar.

So what happens down there?

Holding his breath, Gadol dove straight down. Far enough from the coast that he was sure it was deep water, he plunged through the waves, straight down into the sea. Tucking his wings in tight, he tried different things and discovered he could move through the water fairly well by moving as a snake would.

He also discovered food. Something swam past and he turned and swallowed it, almost on instinct. Suddenly he understood the process that would keep him alive, and eagerly sought out more of the silver morsels.

Eventually tiring of that effort, and having satisfied the craving in his belly, Gadol returned to the surface. Bursting through the waves, he ascended.

Clouds had rolled in, blanketing the sky with grey and misty white. He steadily rose, the sun now stabbing, now glimmering through solid or shredded banks of drifting clouds, until he passed the first layer. A wide view awaited him above, orange from the desert dust and obscured in the distance with plains of rolling, soft clouds underneath him. Higher he flew, suddenly rising above the dust. Clear blue skies opened up around and above him. Far above, thin layers of cirrus marked the end of moisture; beyond that, the air would gradually disappear and the vacuum of the universe would dominate. No longer could he go there, bound by his body of flesh and its need for oxygen, food, and sleep.

Not yet.

The enormous sun above him turned the clouds below into searing white and baked his skin. On he flew, and on, but the cloudbanks below him seemed endless, and he could see nothing. The air grew colder; this must be north, he thought.

If the planet rotates in the normal direction.

Weary muscles begged for relief, and he reluctantly decided to turn back. Just then he saw a bit of snow and a black, jagged rock piercing the heavy blanket of clouds below him. Swooping down, he circled the mountain and found an open place to land -- an island in a sea of cold fog, but a place to rest before returning south. He set down on hard rock with no soil or gravel to get a grip on. Sliding on the damp shale, he tumbled into a crevice and fell hard on his right side. Snarling, bitter thoughts ran through his mind. He hated the planet and the One who had put him here.

He climbed out of the pit, favoring a leg obviously bruised but not broken. On the sloping rock where he stood nothing offered a possibility of either food or water. Further below, on a steeper slope, some gravel softened the sheer bleakness of the place, but there was no evidence of any growth at all. A few steps further and the mountain disappeared into wet, drifting clouds. He had no desire to wander into that soup.

Testing his wings for strain, he found them only weary, not damaged, so he spread them and took to the air again, heading for home. Such as it was.

When he finally reached the cliffs and cave of his awakening he stumbled inside and fell into the sleep of sheer exhaustion.

The next time he awoke it was morning and the sky was clear. After a long drink from the pool and a leisurely breakfast cruising in the waves nearby, he rose into the air for a better look at the planet. Past the cliffs, above the nearby peaks, into the coppery sky. Little enough lived in the sea, and nothing on land; what lived up here? Were there any birds, insects, anything? Were any more of Leviathan's offspring here?

Higher he rose, now circling as the air grew thinner and flying was more difficult. Searching the sky for miles around, he saw nothing. He looked down and realized the planet was truly barren. No indication of vegetation met his eye in any direction.

The simmering hatred of God that always ran like acid in his veins now boiled. A prison planet, indeed, with just enough food in the sea to keep him alive! Forgetting that such provision was a gift, and that the treatment he had earned with his rebellion was far worse, his heart raged.

Higher and higher he rose, to the very limits that the disappearing air would allow. Straining, closer and closer to the blackness of deep space, closer to the realms that were his playground and refuge before the war. Coasting at the limit of his ability to breathe, he yearned to be up there again among the stars. Finally, exhausted, he began drifting down towards the planet's surface.

And he heard his name.

"Now I have a question for you!"

Surprised, I looked up from my embarrassment. "I'll try." What in the world could he have to ask me?

"What are the cords we must loose?"

Silence among the group. We were intensely interested in that question!

"Too bad! I was hoping you knew! I guess we'll find out together."

He gathered us around a marble table at the center of the courtyard set with bowls of fruit and steaming fresh bread. Spread across the table was a map of the constellation Orion as we had always seen it from Earth. Around each star were circles, each with a dot and a word placed somewhere on the circle. Their planets! The planets, and some of the stars, had names I didn't recognize. Alnitak I knew; one of its planets, circled in red, was labelled 'Nsol.

"Father delights in our creativity, so He often adopts the way we have represented things. You remember he told Adam to name the animals? Whatever Adam called them, that became their names."

He pointed to the map. "So He considers Orion to look like this, just the way it looked to us. Obviously, from anywhere else in the universe these stars would form an entirely different pattern, but you'll find this is the view assumed by the angels as well as by us."

He touched the star at the left end of Orion's belt.

"Alnitak is where we're headed. Linus, you may have heard it called 'An-nitaq.' Of course, men could not see well enough to find and name its planets, but it has several. We'll be on this one at first" -- he pointed -- "the one called 'Nsol."

We looked at the map, tracing the circles, wondering what we would find there.

"In many solar systems Father has placed a planet at precisely the distance from that star to support life. Now ..."

He paused, looking around at our faces.

"Now those planets are waiting. It is our job to move out into the universe and carry out the original plan."

"Our job? The four ... five ... of us?" I exclaimed.

Job laughed. "No, not just us. Adam's sons, all of them! Earth was the starting point, but it was never the end of the plan, only the beginning."

Linus shook his head. "Of course. That's always been His way. Start small, light a fire that can't be quenched, and let it grow! We should have known this was coming!"

Julia laughed. "Just like in Ireland. He lit a fire there, and we started out across Britain and into Gaul, spark by spark, pushing back the darkness."

Talk about pushing back the darkness! Deep space. The universe. Good thing we have eternity to get it done!

"How do we get there?" John appeared to be quietly thinking it through, and had gotten one step ahead of us. "Where are we now, in relation to ... well, to any place in the universe, for that matter?"

"My guess is that we're one step away," Job answered. "I think He'll just open a door for us and we'll step into that world."

"How do we get back?" Again, John was thinking far ahead of the rest of us.

"Guess we'll find out when it's time to come back," Linus offered. "I figure we'll operate there just like we did on earth... just like He did. Watching Father and doing what He does!"

Job smiled and looked up at him.

"Tell us about that, Linus - about watching Father, and doing what He does. You know my story, of course. Tell me yours."

Job settled into a carved marble chair hung with scarlet cloth panels and decorated with intricately stitched or woven cushions that blazed with vines and flowers.

"Mine?" said Linus. "Not much to tell. I was in Rome, got to meet Paul. Pretty obvious what happens, when you meet Paul -- you meet Jesus next! Changed my life, and lots of others, too. The number grew rapidly. We learned to pray and to set people free from … from all sorts of things, really. That's what I mean. Just like Jesus did in Jerusalem: listen, watch, obey.

"And eventually, we learned to hide. There was a lot of idolatry and cruelty in the city. There were a lot of wounded people. So we saw lots of healing, lots of deliverance."

"How did you meet him?" asked Julia.

"Paul?"

She nodded.

"We'd been visiting the synagogue, my father and I. Just listening, thinking about their ideas, their faith, and the news from Jerusalem, the amazing things they said had happened there.

"You had to worship Caesar then, and after that whatever else you liked, that was fine. But Caesar was just a man, no more. A fool could see it, but no one could say it, of course.

"But we thought there had to be more. More than Caesar and the temple idols.

"And the gods - Artemis, that Ephesus pushed, any of them, just stories, just fancy tales anyone might make up.

"But the Jews - they were different. They had something that was real. We couldn't figure it out, though. All those rules, all the things you had to do to please God. Didn't seem like God cared as much about all that as they did, from the stories.

"And where was the power? None of our synagogue friends were about to float an axe-head down at the river! Or anything else that happened in their old stories!

"But they knew Him, through all that. They honored something worth honoring -- more than I could say for the rest of us!

"Then Paul came. In chains, at first, and always with a guard.

"We heard he wanted a day at the synagogue to explain about the recent happenings in Jerusalem. Sounded like a storm had blown through that city, and he was fresh from it, so we made sure to be there.

"Not much to look at, Paul. Have you met him yet? You'll see. And not a strong speaker, not loud like the ones you heard in the public squares or in the city meetings.

"But he knew Him! He knew God like no one I ever met.

"And the synagogue - oh, they got stirred up! Some could hardly listen without pacing and muttering and interrupting. And others - Father and me, too - could not hear enough. We strained to hear him over the grumbling of the old beards.

"Because he was sure, absolutely sure. Like a man who's seen something and knows he saw it. May not understand what he's seen, and there were things Paul was still sorting out -- but he was sure, nonetheless, sure enough that he was hanging his whole life on it.

"So they couldn't argue. They'd say, 'That's impossible!' He'd just shrug and say, 'It happened.' Or he would point them to a Scripture and explain that God had told them years ago He would do this, and walk it out for them, step by step, in the ancient writings.

"But you could read those prophets differently, and they were good at that. Some of them would rather argue than eat or sleep, I think.

"So Paul would let them object and complain and threaten, and then he'd take a drink and open a new topic.

"Made them very upset, many of them. But a few listened. Like us.

"Then the synagogue was about to split up. It got so bad, Paul couldn't teach there any longer. Too much anger.

"He rented a house from Claudius, I think, the butcher, and settled in. We almost lived there, we went so often! And you couldn't wear him out! We'd wear out our ears before he wore out his voice!

"I think that's why he spoke so softly, and a little rough - doing that for years would use up anyone's throat! But like I said, he knew God. It was like God had opened up the old writings and said, 'Paul, here's what I meant. Here's where I explained it. Here's where I told you this was coming.'

"Because Paul, you know, used to be one of those angry Jews. Never met Jesus, and was so contemptuous that he wouldn't go hear Him when he heard Jesus was in Jerusalem. Figured he was just an ignorant troublemaker likely to get the city upset like other pot-stirrers had done.

"And he didn't believe the miracle stories. Thought those who did were fools, naive, gullible.

"Then came that trip to Damascus when God knocked him down, blinded him, and turned his head around.

"Must have been amazing, to go back through the books he knew so well -- maybe had memorized, even -- and discover he had never understood them after all. And had memorized all the wrong parts!"

We all laughed.

"What was that 'thorn' he talked about?" I asked. "I've never heard anything I believed was right, and he didn't really explain it in his letter to Corinth."

The others glanced at each other and smiled.

"You'll have to ask him," Linus said with a wink. "I'll tell you this much -- he was amused that it became such a guessing game for God's people for all those years!

Three

Everyone was quiet for a moment. "What about you?" Job turned to me. "How did you come to Father?"

I thought back.

"In my time, the church was doing good things, but I can't say they were 'watching Father, and doing what they saw Him doing.' We read about what you did, long before, and we really wanted that kind of relationship with God, wanted to know Him that way. But most of the church just did good things and tried to be helpful… and met to sing, and pray, and study.

"But we were dissatisfied, at least some of us. There was such a difference between our lives and yours! Between our experience and yours. We wanted it to happen to us, what had happened to you, what we read in Paul's letters, and what John wrote, and Mark. All of it. Miracles, people healed, demons thrown out. And when we went to God about it, He lit the fire. Whoo! That's when things got interesting! We started seeing Him at work, and got moving!"

John nodded. "I wish I could have seen it." He shook his head. "I missed so much."

I looked at him.

"I didn't make it out of the womb," he said quietly. "Never took a breath in that body."

Julia punched him. "You didn't miss anything. That was just practice. Preparation! He was knocking off the rough spots, getting us ready. We were just spending time in school, writing our lessons over and over. This is the time we were preparing for! I guess you just didn't need all those hours sitting on a hard bench, enduring a mean teacher, and meeting the bully on the wagon path!"

John looked at her for a moment. "So the real issue was … all of you needed a head start!"

We all laughed. I was glad for her easy ways.

"Job." Linus was looking at him intently. "What will we face, on 'Nsol? Has He told you?"

Job pulled some bread apart. We savored the warm, fresh smell as it broke free and surrounded us. Taking a big bite, he looked at Linus.

"Is anyone else there?" Linus continued. "And do we have other things to do while we sort out this thing about the cords?"

"Yes," Job replied, "we have things to do." And then, quietly, looking more serious than I had seen him so far, he added, "I think we will have company."

"You worried, you big bear?" Julie challenged Linus. She had a way of putting it on the table, laid out and ready to serve.

"Me?" Linus smiled, then chuckled, and then laughed, a big, deep laugh, with a smile that lit up the garden.

"Not much worried me back there, once I met Him. And now that we're here ... worried?" He laughed again, and suddenly his mirth gave way to unconstrained joy, and the floodgates were open. He tried manfully to stop, and wiped his eyes, but looking around at us all he began laughing all the more. And the more he laughed, the more it pulled us in and bundled us along, until we all fell against each other, caught up in it, helpless, with our tears streaming down.

"Job," I said, when I could, "I've got to tell you ... there was a song about you. Listen to this, about your friends who offered such poor comfort in your distress!"

And in my best imitation of Don Francisco, I sang it for them:

"We'll give you cold comfort, though we say we're your friends,
we don't know what you've done, but still we're sure that you've sinned!
We'll give you cold comfort, 'cause we've made up our minds,
and when you know that you're right, there ain't no need to be kind!"

"Wait," I said, laughing. "I've got to get to the next line!"

"Even if you're ignorant of what you did wrong,
We can pile on some guilt! Yes, we can help you along!
If death, loss, and sickness still have not made a dent,
We'll beat you with our words until you finally repent!"

Job fell apart, and his laughter pulled us all into it with him.
Finally, we recovered.
What a time we'll have, I thought. What a time.
"And as for what needs doing out there," Job continued, when we could listen, "you might talk to Adam, and see if he has any advice for us! We may be working a garden twice the size of the Earth. It's time for 'Nsol to blossom!"

'Athaq brooded quietly, in the depths of Alnitak. The heat at the center of the star made no difference to him, nor the pressures, nor the blinding light, nor the all-obliterating roar of continual nuclear fusion. It was a place to hide and think and plan, as the holocaust around him generated a blistering stream of overpowering energy in all directions. The star and he were one in some way only the Creator understood. Placed here eons ago to shepherd this part of the physical universe, this was the center of his domain, his part of the created Universe, and he left only when he and the other Watchers were called to assemble before the One.

He knew it was time for Adam's sons to come and thought he knew their mission. As far as he surmised, their stewardship superseded his own, but they would be concerned with planets, not stars, and he cared not for the planets.

So Job would be coming. How interesting.

He remembered well the time they gathered at the Throne, and Lucifer came among them to challenge God's goodness, and the time of Job's trial began. What a strange thing for the One to allow to happen to one who loved Him. Strange indeed His ways, even to the spirits. And now, these sons of Adam, in whom He has hidden his plans for eternity, were coming. Coming to his constellation, Orion. Coming to his home, Alnitak. And that meant coming to 'Nsol, the planet so obviously positioned perfectly for man - with the temperature, and the seasons, and the atmosphere they would enjoy.

He turned his mind to 'Nsol and the act of thought became motion through the plasma and outward. The star felt him leaving. A violent nuclear plume rose from the surface, wrapping him in its blistering fingers until he was well on his way towards the planet. As he had ignored the steel-vaporizing heat within Alnitak, he now ignored the deadly cold surrounding him, moving far beyond light-speed as he crossed the solar system.

The man who endured everything Lucifer could do to him, yet stayed faithful, was coming to 'Nsol. Did he know that Livya-Gadol was there? Could he guess the ancient venom that bubbled in Gadol's veins, the depth of his hatred?

The planet rushed to meet him. Bare rock, huge sandy plains, raw mountains stretching up to icy caps. What would it be when Job finished his task?

Coming to the surface, he allowed a sonic boom to announce his arrival. Livya-Gadol had finally awakened, and it was time for 'Athaq to establish his supervisory role over him.

As it turned out, Adam was delighted to know we were going. I could not believe I was talking with Job, much less Adam!

"But your role will be different than mine."

We waited, as he was silent for a moment, apparently lost in thought.

"I was just a man, watching what He was doing. And being amazed at His creativity, of course. Have you seen those things that grow under the seas?"

I was the only one who guessed what he was talking about. "Like the fish with a lantern on the end of its nose?"

"Yes!" he laughed. "How strange!"

"But," he continued, "I think He wants you to have a more active role. After all, you're twice-born. I was not."

I remembered another scripture that had fascinated me: "When we see Him, we will be like Him…"

"Exactly." Job smiled. "Our model is not Adam, but Jesus. When our first-born Brother walked in our shoes, how did He interact with the physical world?"

I thought about it.

"My task was to ask, and watch, and name the creation as he brought it forth, and tend it," suggested Adam. "Yours will be to understand His will, and -- if I see what's happening -- command it to come forth!"

John had not read the Bible, so he could not have known the stories I grew up with. "How does that work?"

"Well, when Jesus did it, sometimes it happened right then ... sometimes not," I said. "He told a storm to quiet, and it did. But he told a fig tree to wither, and it didn't change until the next day."

"That's faster than most of us changed, when He told us to!" laughed Julia. "I think that fig tree was doing pretty well!"

"Well," said Linus, deadpan, "it couldn't run away and hide from His voice, like some would do."

Julia stared at him without cracking a smile.

"I mean … it was planted. It couldn't move!"

"Oh," she replied, with a twinkle in her eye. "So, you didn't mean anything personal?"

"No, of course not!" he said. "Except for you, of course," he added under his breath. Julia punched him, and he grabbed his arm, crying out, "What? What did I say?"

"Nothing," she said. "Nothing at all."

"Adam," I ventured. "How did you think of names for everything?"

He laughed. "So many creatures, all so different! I tried to sense their nature, almost to ask them what their names were, if I could tell. Then I just offered something that seemed right, something that seemed to fit."

"To ask them …?" John probed.

"That was before my sin," Adam replied. "When I still had Dominion. Before I let it … slip away."

We nodded.

"There was a bond between us and the created beings. It was quickly lost, but you will experience that on the new planets!"

I tried to imagine what that would be like.

"So, I have a question." Job was always taking us off the map.

"Did the original sin stain the whole universe, all of creation? Or just Earth?"

Adam smiled. The rest of us were silent.

"And did His sacrifice heal that for the Universe, or just for Earth?" I asked.

"Will the planet you go to, and the new life you bring forth, be tainted?" Adam asked.

I wondered the same thing.

Gadol emerged, irritated at the brutal interruption of his sleep and momentarily blinded by 'Athaq's presence. It was just after midnight, he guessed. Although night and day meant nothing to 'Athaq, Gadol was now dealing with the realities of living in a physical world. He found that sudden intrusions of blinding light and deafening sound blasts, bringing him out of deep sleep and sour dreams, were not to his liking.

Neither was this intruder.

They faced each other, as Gadol's eyes narrowed and adapted to the brilliance into which he stared.

"I know what you are. Which one are you?" demanded Gadol.

"I have been charged with watching over you, as you consider the Rebellion, the part you played, and where your allegiance will lie in the future."

"My keeper." Gadol snorted the word with derision. "Think you have a leash that can hold me?"

'Athaq thought about Leviathan, magnificent and powerful, and what a poor, twisted, angry copy of that magnificence now crouched before him. Kin to Leviathan, no doubt. One of the "sons of Pride," cast down. The resemblance was startling, even after the creature had been reduced to physical form and stripped of the jeweled scales and overwhelming force of presence his kind had radiated in the spiritual realm. 'Athaq began to wonder if this arrogant, unrepentant creature might be of some use to him.

"Do I have a leash that can hold you?"

'Athaq reached out. An appendage of pure light, excruciating in its brightness, hovered over Gadol and slowly descended: slowly, slowly, irresistibly it came down. Gadol was pressed down onto the rock, and pressed, and pressed. Flattening out under the unrelenting weight, he could at length draw no air into his lungs, and still the squeeze increased. At the point of being crushed, when even his heartbeat could find no space to continue, the pressure stabilized. When 'Athaq judged that the agony of his victim had become unbearable, the light vanished and the pressure was gone.

"Yes. I do."

Gasping for air, his lungs heaving, Gadol rose. He stretched up to his full height, rage contorting his face, and towered over his visitor. 'Athaq turned away in a calculated show of bored disrespect that he knew would leave Gadol suddenly cold and empty, and perhaps for the first time in his very long life, helpless.

'Athaq turned back to face him as Gadol sank to the ground.

"Livya-Gadol. A strong name -- 'insolent, great, mighty, boastful.' It fit you well. How far you have fallen."

Gadol glowered at him, obviously seething.

"Visitors are coming. They may not know you are here. You may want to hide."

Suddenly Gadol was alone, and deep darkness engulfed him. His eyes adjusted. The stars slowly regained their midnight glory across the heavens above him. But his keeper was gone. Apparently.

He tried to sleep, but twisted and rolled and dreamed of things he hated until the heat of a desert morning forced him to the water. Who were the visitors that were coming? Why would his "Keeper" warn him? Why should he hide?

Deep under the pounding waves, searching out the fish that were his maddeningly consistent diet, Gadol noticed that underwater caves riddled the cliffs. He chose one of the larger holes and dove into the blackness. After smashing his head into a protruding rock he backed off and waited. Slowly, dimly, the path through the rocks emerged from the pitch black around it, and his adjusting eyes could guide him deeper within. A hundred feet, two hundred feet, and the feel of the water changed. He drifted upwards and broke free into a chamber of air. Not trusting himself to fly, for fear of rocks that could be inches above, he probed the edges of the cavern under water until he found a gravel slope rising from the water.

Gadol climbed upon the gravel, and felt no barrier. He pitched rocks high into the air and they struck nothing. He growled into the air and heard the echo of a large space in front of him.

He walked forward, climbing a broad and easy slope. Coming up a steep bank, he found that it leveled off. How far did it go? He slowly moved forward in pitch blackness, taking careful steps, finding no resistance. Snarling into the void, his sound echoed back from a distance, and echoed in multiple waves. Caverns? Many of them?

Moving carefully, he suddenly bumped into a wall. He felt of it. The wall seemed more a corner than an end. Which way? Again he roared into the inky emptiness and listened. His voice echoed back quickly from the left, but not for several seconds from the right. He turned right.

Hours later, after probing as much as he dared without losing track of the way back, he lay on the gravel bank and thought. This could be useful. But he would need light. If those visitors were a problem, he could bring them here, and do what he wished with them. Slowly. Mmm, that was the first pleasurable thought to cross his mind in a long time. He slept.

He awoke some unknown time later, to a moment of panic. Was he blind? Why could he see nothing?

Memory returned. Memory of the underwater cavern, of hours without sight as he explored it. He could smell the water close by, and crawled into it, letting the coolness refresh him. Sinking into it, he began harvesting bites of silver and white as they swam by, at first just by smell, but as he moved towards the undersea cliff opening and the filtered, faint light of the brilliant night sky, he could gather them more quickly. Bursting forth from the cavern's opening, he pushed up to the surface and spread his grey, rough wings.

What a pity, he thought. I was brilliant. I was blinding, when I sparkled before the throne.

The throne. Angry, frustrated thoughts flooded his heart, and he turned straight up. There's got to be someone else. There's got to be a way out of this nonsense, this prison, this eternity of absolutely nothing.

Soaring to the height of his ability, he listened, listened, listened. Finally, he heard it again. His name, being called from a great distance. But not in a voice he was eager to hear.

To respond would be to make himself known to one he hated. Not to respond would be worse.

Four

The Watchers assembled before the throne in response to a call only they could hear.

The angels moved back, honoring these that the One called the 'Sons of God'. Not physical, like his Son and those made in his image, crowned with glory and honor even in their corruption. Not like Melchizedek, the priest and king with no beginning or end, priest by the power of indestructible life. And not like them. Shepherds, of a sort. Living in the stars, looking after portions of the physical universe. Guardians.

Perhaps that was it, thought Gabriel, as he watched them come before the throne one by one. Guardians. Keeping things, until those appointed are ready to take possession.

His eye was caught by one in particular. Something seemed wrong. 'Athaq stood there, from Alnitak, where Livya-Gadol was kept. Always reserved, 'Athaq seemed more so at this moment, even moody.

"As you know," said the One, when all had offered their greetings and reverence, "Lucifer once stood here among you and requested permission to torment my servant Job."

Yes, they remembered. Who could not remember? Gabriel stirred, recalling the events. Job had been known and revered in all the earth, and Lucifer's brutal treatment reduced him to a shredded, tormented soul, rejected and despised by his close friends and even his wife. Yes, they remembered.

"It has begun."

All were silent. They knew what He meant.

"Job is the first, and those with him. Others will go out as well. The sons of Adam will bring to full bloom the planets prepared for them, the solar systems you have kept for them these long years."

'Athelkan stepped forward.

"What about Leviathan's kin?"

All murmured. Many of the Dominant would stand against any such visitors.

"Watch over the sons of Adam," He replied, "as they come to you." The tenderness in His voice was a delight to hear, and His love for His children saturated His words. "You have been faithful. Welcome them, and watch over them with me."

A lilting melody of praise began among the angels surrounding them, and the Watchers added their silvery voices to the chorus.

Jesus would continue his service before the throne, Gabriel realized, interceding for his brothers and ministering to his Father in a relationship the angels could only marvel at. But his brothers, those redeemed from all the ages of Earth by his sacrifice, would now begin their long-awaited stewardship of the galaxies that awaited them.

A glorious moment, thought Gabriel. He remembered going to Mary, and her response, when God introduced His Son into her womb. The second Adam, the one who reclaimed the title deed to all creation from the usurper, and put the Plan back in motion. And now it had begun.

A glorious moment indeed.

The beauty of Creation was astounding already; what would it become as Adam's redeemed race stepped into their true rule, as they finally took Dominion?

Gadol plunged into the waves, ready to escape the intolerable heat and see what really lay underneath the mountain.

Swimming slowly, grabbing silver bites when convenient, he explored the undersea cliff face. Many openings appeared to be just crevices, offering no deeper access into the mountain, and many holes were smaller than his body could pass.

Finally he found the cave he had entered on his first dive. Returning to the surface for more air, he circled lazily up a few hundred feet, then folded his wings and fell, spearing the foam and disappearing into the sea.

He turned towards the mountain and moved slowly into the underwater cave. He knew now to avoid the outcrops, to weave a path through jagged obstacles.

He came to the gravel slope that rose from the water and opened into black, cold, stale air.

"This will not do," he thought. He rose carefully into the air and sought the walls, then followed them up to the ceiling. Finding the highest point, Gadol began focusing his breath on the ceiling. The rock began melting. Molten iron dripped on him. Disgusted and scalded, he dropped back into the water a hundred feet below to cool down.

"Where am I?" he wondered. "What is above this?" He sank down to the depths. Emerging minutes later into the turbulence of the open sea, he rose to the surface and noted a white scar on the cliff face that would serve as a marker. Sweeping up into the air, he rose in a tight circle to land on the cliff above his underwater entrance.

He moved inland and realized the cave he had awakened in was approximately over the underwater cavern. If he bored a hole in this direction, then punched up a chimney …

He entered the darkness and moved to the back of the cave.

"I may want another way out of there, too," he muttered, and began stirring up his anger and hatred, thinking of those who had wronged him. His blood soon reached the temperature he sought. Smoke began seeping from his mouth and nose. A yellow light shone in his eyes. Choosing a likely spot, he roared at the wall, and a hole appeared, big enough for him to walk into. In a few moments the air cleared of the vaporized rock. He stepped forward and did it again. When the heat and smoke were too much, he returned to the pool and refreshed himself, then took it up again. After an hour, he judged the tunnel to be long enough. He turned down, and began boring into the rock.

Livya-Tontal stormed along the gravel beach on 'Nsela's equator, cursing the four suns beating down on him and the empty lands around him. Waste of a planet! Surely someone else is awake by now!

Tonight, when the air cooled, when he could fly the highest, when those blistering suns were not cooking his eyes and skin. Tonight he would try again. He would not spend eternity walking this barren rock, alone and raging. Not if he could get away.

Leaping into the air at midnight, he opened his huge wings and thrashed the air to climb. Higher, higher, above the few paltry clouds and up towards the orange and yellow moons. Even at night the relentless winds swept in from the sea, boiling up under him, pushing him away from the surface. Even the planet hated him!

Up, up, beyond where he could fly with any comfort, past all the atmosphere he could put behind him. Up where the air was so thin that breathing was hard, but past all possible resistance to reaching out.

Finally, he coasted on almost nothing, far above the rocks and surf and wretched deserts of his prison planet, with millions of stars blazing just out of reach. And he called.

Before they were cast down, before they were judged for the failure of Lucifer and condemned with him, before they were trapped in these ridiculous physical bodies and thrown across the universe into these rocky wastelands, before all that, when they were beautiful, and mighty, and free, before … they could speak to each other then, across the heavens, across any distance, mind to mind, spirit to spirit. Maybe they still could. Maybe.

"Gadol!" he called. "Gadol, are you there? Wake up, you wretched insect!"

A deep silence answered him.

"Ruunt! Answer me!"

Nothing.

"Guntel!"

The stars mocked him, pretending they could not hear him and he could no longer hear the music to which they danced. The blackness above him teemed with invisible life, and ignored him.

Absolute isolation swept in and crushed him again, a desperate sense of being totally alone among all the myriad life forms he knew were out there, physical and not. It was not a loneliness for companionship, for his heart desired no such thing, but a need for something to control, something to beat into submission. A need for things to oppress and use and destroy. A need for victims and slaves. A need for power.

"Tontal?"

Faint, but unmistakable. There it was! Gadol was alive and awake, finally.

"Where are you?" called Tontal, sending his thought across the light-years with all the energy he could focus into it, though weary with the effort of staying this high with so little air to lift him. "Talk to me, worm! Where are you?"

Minutes passed. Gadol must have fallen back into the atmosphere, and needed to climb back to the edges of sustainable flight to respond. Eventually, the response came, faint but clear.

"'Nsol. Near Alnitak. 'Athaq is here. I can't …"

Tontal heard no more, even after calling repeatedly and enduring all the lung-sucking vacuum he could stand. Exhausted, he relaxed and fell, plunging straight down towards the planet, then turning into wide, drifting circles to coast down without the scorching heat of friction adding to his smoldering anger. Weakling! Couldn't even stay up long enough to set a time to connect again! Waste of flesh, never mind spirit.

He dove into the churning waves surrounding the mountainous island he had chosen as home. Sweeping through the salty, bitter water, he ate all the fish his belly would hold. Small fish, nothing big enough for a decent bite, never mind a meal. Wretched place. Miserable planet.

He turned up, broke the surface and glided to the coast, landing yards from a crevice into the mountain's heart that led to his protected lair. Purely from habit he listened for a moment, then moved silently into the opening and into the cavern that sloped down into the roots of the mountain.

Tomorrow night. Same time. The planet must have turned towards 'Nsol. Surely that wretch would think the same thing, and return to the heights to try again.

'Athaq was there?

He stopped, frozen with the thought.

'Athaq. The one Watcher that would surely be a rebel. The one he could work with, if there were any. Not trust, never that, but he could find common ground with 'Athaq, long enough to use him. And try not to be used in return.

'Athaq. Very interesting. Tomorrow he would try to reach 'Athaq.

Throwing himself down in a shallow pool, he slept, and in his dreams he called endlessly into an empty universe.

We gathered in the courtyard, all at the same time as though called. I suppose we all felt it. A tension held me, and a tingling anticipation that today was the beginning of an adventure I could not even imagine.

Job emerged from the house, boots and rough fabric pants in place of the sandals and robe he'd always worn. It was true. We were leaving.

"Let's take food," he suggested. "Pack for a week or so. By that time I think we'll have other sources of things to eat, but ..."

"Is it a desert?" asked Linus.

"Probably just empty," offered John. "New."

I tried to imagine such a thing. An empty planet? New?

"And wear long sleeves. Take a hat," Job added. "It's a different sun than we were used to -- a couple of them. It will be hotter and brighter. Might take some getting used to."

Julie caught John's eye, and winked. It would be the first planet he walked on, not the second. He smiled.

We dispersed to gather belongings and prepare. At dusk we met Job in the courtyard where I had first seen him, and I sampled another of his sweet, crunchy apples. Jolina was there, offering food and drink for all.

"I'll miss this, and your hospitality!" I told her. She hugged me, and her quick smile was a blessing in itself. "Be praying for you!" she said, with an obvious confidence in Job, and in us, that put a joy in my heart. "Likewise," I said, "if Job gives us any time for such things!"

"How much time do you need?" asked Julia, with a nudge and that infectious grin. "Eternity's not enough?"

"Maybe not. I'll try to make do!"

Job gathered us at the gate onto the stunningly beautiful boulevard outside, and we walked alongside towering oaks, or something very like oaks, waving at the friends we passed.

"Linus! Is that Cornelius, the one Peter went to see? Over there!"

Linus looked back. "Might be. He favors red, and the white trim looks familiar, too. When we get back I'll introduce you!"

"Please. I want some serious time with him!"

"What is it with you and time?" laughed Julia. "Do we need to get you a watch, or a clock, or something?"

Job chuckled. "I've got one you can use. Big flat surface with a triangle standing up in the middle. Heavy to carry, though…"

"I'm good, I'm good. No problem!"

"Good thing," added John. "I've seen it. Wouldn't fit in your pack!"

We reached the nearest gate out onto the meadows surrounding our homes. As we emerged into the brilliant greens of the hillside and riotous color of the wild flowers, a white horse and a familiar rider galloped up the hill to meet us, hair blowing and the joy of Life itself apparent in his every movement.

"Friends, are you ready?" He called.

Jumping down, He embraced us each, speaking a few words of instruction, encouragement, whatever He felt we needed. To me he said, "Remember. Life now is lived just like it was on Earth: led by the Spirit, we do what Father does, and say what Father says, and live by faith, not sight. Believe, and trust, and take the adventure! I'm always with you." The warmth of his smile filled me, and I embraced him.

"Oh, by the way," He added, "you won't be flying around there. And you'll be visible. You had fun in the clouds and river, didn't you?"

"Yes, thank you!"

He smiled, and I knew he shared my pleasure.

He stepped back, blessed us, and leapt onto the bare back of the stallion. As He bade us farewell, He and the meadows disappeared, as though a cloud had settled over us.

What a cloud! Bright, golden bright, crackling with energy, pulsing with the presence of Life Himself.

Perhaps this was what they felt in Jerusalem, when they dedicated the first Temple and God himself came to fill it. Or some faint shadow of this, perhaps. Although the account said it overwhelmed them, and none could do their tasks! I believe it. If I were still in the old flesh, I doubt I could have stayed on my feet!

When it faded away, we looked around. I was stunned by the emptiness and oppressive heat. Barren rock and desert surrounded us, with hills and further mountains towards ... towards what? Where was North, here? None of the old clues would help!

A giant sun beat down on us from directly overhead, and a smaller one drifted over the horizon ahead of us. We squinted, and waited while our eyes adjusted.

"The big one is Alnitak," said Job. "Twenty times the size of the sun we knew."

In front of us a stream flowed lazily by, making its way from the mountains far to our left and meandering into the hazy distance on the right. When we could see again, I walked over to it, sat down, and took my boots off.

"Feet sore? Did I miss something? Have we actually walked yet?"

"No, Julia, as far as I know!" I replied, "But that water looks great!" I climbed down the shallow, rocky bank and slipped into the knee-deep water. Cool, perfectly clear, moving gently past my feet, it was delightful. But something was wrong.

I lifted a handful to my mouth. Sweet, fresh water. But …

"There's nothing in it! No fish, no leaves, no … nothing. Nothing at all!"

They nodded, watching. The total absence of all living things would take some getting used to, coming from the center of Life itself.

"Shh. Listen."

I heard it too. Job had caught the sound of surf in the distance to our right.

"Let's go see," said Julia. "Any reason to go another direction? Might be a place there to find some shelter… and a more interesting landscape than this!"

"You know, a truly empty world is oppressive," I said.

"No life at all. No green on the hillsides, no bees, no birds, no sound at all," agreed Julia. "Just our boots crunching on the sand and rock."

A hot breeze pushed us forward, bringing dust from the desert to collect in our hair and down our collars. We walked.

The smaller sun had apparently been in the west, or so we now called it, as it disappeared early in our walk, falling below the horizon ahead of us and a little to our left. The larger one followed. As the surf grew louder, the ground rose around us, becoming more rocky and difficult to climb. The stream we followed cut deeper into the rock, and became a narrow, foamy rush of water eager for the sea. We tramped alongside on gravel banks and shoals, the cliffs rising higher on either side.

By the time we reached a view of the ocean, massive Alnitak sat on the horizon ahead of us, fiery red through the low atmosphere and setting a torch to the distant waters. A few brave stars pushed through the deepening blue above, announcing a teeming starfield to come. The sound of rolling waves seemed almost upon us when we discovered a cave with a wide pool and something of a sandy beach in front of it.

"Perhaps a place to stow some things?" suggested Job.

We entered slowly. Linus led the way. The rock under our feet offered no trace of prints from creatures going in and out.

"There wouldn't be any," said Julia, as I searched the ground. "There's nothing here to leave tracks."

"Right. I keep forgetting."

We eased into the cave, letting our eyes adjust.

"Think anything lives here?"

"No, John, I don't think anything lives anywhere!" laughed Julia.

Linus was further inside than the rest of us, and stopped abruptly.

"Something does."

We froze.

"Smell that?"

I did. Acrid, moldy, sour. Something had spent many hours in here, maybe years. But none of it smelled fresh, and there was no sound whatsoever.

"I think it's gone," said Linus.

Job came in from exploring a bit more around the cave opening. He lifted a hand and began painting light onto the walls, a light that moved from his hand to the walls like paint from a latex brush. Moving along the wall, holding his glowing palm about seven feet up and inches away from the rock, he steadily lit the entire cave with a soft orange glow.

We watched in amazed delight.

"Oh," he said, finally noticing his audience and mocking a small bow. We applauded.

"Do you like that? Father gave me a few things to help us get started. Since there are no trees yet, there's no wood, so there's nothing to build with, or to burn for light."

"What else did he send along?" asked John. "Food?"

"Now that you remind me…"

Job set his pack down, untied the silky blue cord, and lifted out a bundle. Unwrapping it, he offered baked bread and apples to all comers.

"From Jolina, actually. She thought we'd appreciate a memento of the garden."

We dropped our packs and hats around the walls of the cave, and set to. Strange to enjoy the tastes of Home in a place so unlike Job's courtyard!

"Well." Job looked around. "Not much to see, here. You're right about something living here, but it seems to have been a while. Shall we look deeper?"

I had noticed an opening at the back; Job led us through it into even deeper night. Again he raised his hand, and light brushed onto the wall as we stooped and ducked and made our way through a winding tunnel, until the floor suddenly dropped away before us.

"Shh…" Job leaned forward, and we listened. "Thought I heard something."

We waited, but heard nothing at all.

John eased forward to the edge, and dropped a handful of gravel into the blackness.

Nothing.

Finally there was a faint echo of gravel on rock, and I thought I heard a bit of a splash as well.

"I'd say our new home has a back door," offered John. "Perhaps our smelly friend made it."

"Perhaps he'll be back," said Julia.

"I think he knows we're here, and won't reveal himself anytime soon," said Job, turning back towards the cave.

"You're not surprised, are you?"

"No, Julia, I suspected we would have company. What I don't know is whose side he's on!"

'Athelkan drifted along the surface of the star Mintaka, undisturbed amidst the violent storms of solar eruptions and the 30,000 degrees that would vaporize anything physical that came near. The dense nuclear violence at the star's heart provided one sort of pleasure, and the much thinner storms and swirls at the surface provided another. From here he could see the hotter star that orbited Mintaka, and the two smaller stars a quarter light-year away that orbited them both.

Something worried him. Livya-Tontal seemed well contained on 'Nsela, the fourth planet out, but he had not visited Tontal for a while, and more unusual, had not heard his violent cursing recently, or his outbursts of anger at being restrained. 'Athelkan could hear such things, in spite of the roar of solar furnace in which he dwelt; it was obviously a tool from the One to monitor his ward.

Was the creature doing something he should not? Finding a possibility of escape? Reaching out, trying to contact others of Leviathan's kin? Was he succeeding? Was it even something to be concerned with?

He decided to pay Tontal a visit.

Livya-Tontal awoke to see white-hot light flooding his lair, though it was deep into the night and he lay a thousand feet from the opening and around many turns of rock. There was only one possibility. That fool Watcher had come to torment him again. Fine, let him wait. Maybe for days.

The light grew brighter, and the cave began to heat. Sweat poured from Tontal, and he realized this was a game he could not play very long.

"All right!" he growled. "I'm coming! Turn off your furnace!"

The heat stopped, and the light faded to a tolerable glare. Tontal stretched, clambered to his feet, and casually made his way to the opening.

"Are you well?"

Tontal snorted in surprise and disgust. What would he care? What would God care? Is that fool still expecting me to repent? Get away from my hole! Hasn't He made me miserable enough yet?

He emerged from the cave. "Until you came."

Silence, as 'Athelkan looked at him, no expression visible.

"You have been quiet."

"You miss my cursing? I'll try to remember that. Didn't know you enjoyed such things."

Again, silence.

"Are we done, Watcher? Have you enjoyed visiting my prison? Are you ready to return to your star, and leave me to rant and suffer?"

"He waits for your change of heart. You were beautiful, and can be again. You were free, and pure spirit. You can be again. You know the choice before you."

Tontal turned away, insulting 'Athelkan with his back.

"He only desires my pain and anguish at being trapped and bound here. My hatred of Him is the only thing greater than His hatred of me. You came to taunt me. That's all you ever come for. Go away."

Darkness fell. After a time, his eyes adjusted, and the star fields emerged above him. His determination to leave this place was complete. There would be a way.

Five

As the heat of a new day seeped into the cave, I woke rested. The pallets we brought weighed almost nothing, but offered an easy rest even on the rocky floor.

"Let's go find that beach," begged Julia, and we all tumbled out to follow her.

The direction was easy to determine, and less than a hundred yards away we found ourselves approaching a mammoth, sheer cliff falling away to rolling surf far below.

"Rocky. No beach here!" said Linus, peering down through the rising salty mist. "But maybe some fishing!"

"Really? You folded up a fishing pole in that pack of yours, and some catfish bait?"

Linus stared at her. "Cat … fish … bait?"

She laughed, and pointed at me. "You'll have to ask him!"

"Oh, yeah, I did tell you about that, didn't I?" I turned to the others.

"May be unique to my part of the world, don't know. There's a fish with long whiskers" - I demonstrated - "that reminds some people of a cat. So … 'catfish'."

Julia began circling around us with her fingers waving, a perfect image of a fish with whiskers.

"And the bait we used to catch it was … awful, actually. It stinks. And you get it on your hands, and then you smell awful too."

"Did you bring any?" asked Job.

"You'd know it, if I had!" I laughed. "You would already know it! And besides," I said, looking out over the waves, "there wouldn't be any catfish down there."

"Actually," said Job, "there's not much of anything down there, until we get busy."

We waited. This could be fun.

"Let's go … there. Up high." Job pointed to the cliffs rising above us. "Let's see how high we can get."

He led us to the foot of the cliffs towering over our cave. "We might want a better view of what happens next," he tossed over his shoulder as he searched for a path up the rock. Linus found it first, a slanting outcrop providing a slope we could climb. "Last one up has to cook breakfast!"

Of course, there was nothing to cook breakfast with, and no breakfast to cook, so none of us wanted that challenge! We scrambled.

Julia came out on the plateau first. After growing up in the hills of Ireland she obviously loved the climbing life, and took to it eagerly. "What a view!" she exclaimed, as we clambered over the last of the cliff face. "Lots and lots of absolutely nothing!"

We stared at the miles of desert over which we had come, bleak and shimmering in the morning heat. "You could cook a stone out there," John murmured.

"So, what shall we do?" asked Job. We all looked at him, having no more idea what to do than how to cook breakfast.

Finally, Linus answered. "What we always do."

"Exactly!" roared Job, grabbing him by both shoulders with an exultant smile. "Exactly!"

"And what … if I may reach a little deeper into your understanding … what do we always do?" I asked.

John and Julia nodded, the same question on their lips.

Job and Linus smiled at us. I think they were enjoying the moment.

"Shall I tell them?" Linus asked.

"Please."

He turned to us and stretched out both hands, palms up. "What do you always do? Think!"

Silence, and then Julia offered the obvious answer. "We walk by faith."

"Right!" said Job. "And when Jesus walked around Israel the first time, how did he do everything? He was showing us, right? How did he do it? When something needed doing, how did he do it?"

We thought about it.

"Well... when something needed doing, he prayed, he understood what the Father had in mind. Then he ... he just said it. He commanded it."

"What about us? Do we know what God wants done here?"

Looking around us, it was abundantly clear what needed doing. Nothing was here yet. The suns, the dry ground, the ocean. Nothing more.

"Let's start with grass," suggested Julia. "Let's soften up the landscape a bit!"

Job nodded. "I like it." Turning to look out over the dry and lifeless landscape before us, Job shouted to the horizon, "Grow! Grass, come forth!"

For hours, we waited. Nothing changed. A peaceful expectancy filled my heart. We had nothing else to do. We waited. The afternoon passed, and we watched as massive Alnitak dropped to the horizon and the deepening blue above us began sparkling with the gems of the unfiltered night sky.

Job whispered, "Could you count the stars? What a promise he made Abraham!"

Linus said, "Remember when Jesus cursed that fig tree, and nothing happened?"

"Until the next day," I said. "Right."

"Well, let's turn in," suggested Job. "It's almost dark, and we may wake up to a whole new world!"

When dawn woke us, I knew instantly the world had changed. A sweet smell filled the cave; the ever-present dust no longer drifted on the breeze. We stepped out into a green world. Ivy climbed the rock next to the entrance. Lush grass covered the ground, stretching out over the plains. Grey and white cumulus clouds, the first we had seen in the sky, drifted overhead, and sheets of silent rain fell in the distance from darker masses. A flash of lightning appeared in the darkest of those, and half a minute later the first thunder rolled across 'Nsol.

"It's begun!" shouted Julia, grabbing Linus by the hands and dancing a happy circle. "Glory!" he shouted back, and lifted her by the waist, spinning around. "Glory!"

I ran to the cliffs over the sea, wondering what might have happened out there. John ran up behind me. "What?" he shouted over the roar of the surf on the rocks. I smiled back at him. "I want to go fishing!" I laughed.

"OK," said Job, coming up behind us. "Do it."

They all looked at me. I turned, looking out over the sea. "Fish! Crustaceans! Whales and dolphins and turtles! All manner of undersea life! Come forth!"

Gadol awoke, curled up on the gravel slope in the underwater cave. His stomach growled. He stretched and slithered into the water to find more of the detested silver morsels. As he drifted out from the black depths under the cliffs, an eel slipped by, and a school of yellow minnows fled before it. Gadol stared. He flexed his long body and moved on through the tunnel towards the open sea. Emerging from the opening under the cliff face, he suddenly pulled back from a passing shark. It swerved at his appearance then glided away into blue-green waters. A ray stirred on the bottom, catching Gadol's eye as it shimmered under the sand.

He looked around, searching the waters as far as he could see. In every direction he caught glimmers of motion. All manner of scales and fins glistened under the rays of light that penetrated this deep into the sea. What had happened? God would not have done this for him, he was sure.

The visitors. Did He do it for them? Had they come?

A flounder drifted by and became breakfast.

Easing to the surface, Gadol peered out, wanting to be found on his own terms, and not yet. No one was in sight. Suddenly it struck him: the cliffs were different. Splotches of green littered the cliff faces and at the top he could see green shrubbery, ferns, tangled ivy, and flowering plants hanging over the side. What had happened?

A movement at the top of the cliff caught his eye. A person stood there; nothing else had that shape. Another came to join the first, then two more. He eased back under water, and drifted motionless. What should he do? If he flew up now, they would see him. He sank into the waves, dove deeper, and gathered more to eat before returning to the cave. Rage suddenly consumed him. Worse than being imprisoned on this planet alone was to have others sent without his knowledge. Without his permission. Wasn't this his planet now? Nothing else lived here, at least until today. This was intolerable. They would pay. God would pay. He would watch them, and see what they were doing, and then ... and then remove them. Use them, if they could do anything for him, and then ... and then get rid of them.

Six

"Did it seem to you that the tunnel back there is not a natural formation?" mused Julia, as we sat resting in the cave.

I thought about it. "Seems a little too even, in its width and height, doesn't it?"

"Yes. And the way it ends ... not in any expected way, but as though it simply turns. Straight down."

"So, if it were made on purpose ... by the creature Job expects to find?"

"Yes."

"And perhaps it's a door from the porch into the main house?"

She laughed. "Exactly."

After a few minutes, she continued.

"Did you run your hand along the wall, as we explored the tunnel?"

"I don't remember."

"Come here," she said, getting up. "Let me show you something."

We walked back to the opening and moved carefully into the tunnel, crouching to enter.

"Feel this."

She reached out to the wall, and dragged her fingers along it. I did the same.

"There are sharp places, and it's ragged overall, but ... the actual rock is smooth, almost glassy in places."

A vague memory stirred. "Melted."

"Maybe so." She nodded, examining the wall closely. "Melted. By what?"

We looked at each other.

"And look at this tunnel, how it's shaped. It's not tall, like a person would make it. It's really as wide as it is tall."

I looked both ways, and realized that even as it turned this way and that, it maintained that approximate shape. And we could see glistening reflections of Job's painted light, as though from an ancient glass wall covered in centuries of dust.

Suddenly I could imagine something rather like a snake, a very big snake, moving quite comfortably through this tunnel.

"Whatever made this is low and long," I said, "and knows how to make a fire."

"A very well-directed fire," she agreed. "And I don't think it was using matches."

Night covered the planet. Gadol once again emerged from the undersea cavern. Breaking the surface, he paused, looking for any sign of the people, and then rose into the air, shaking the water from his wings. Climbing several hundred feet above the cliffs, he circled around behind the cave where he first awoke. He noticed a light seeping from its entrance, and a man standing in that light.

He waited until the man returned into the cave, then drifted down quietly from the back side of the mountain and settled as close to the opening as he could without being seen. The voices inside were clear, and he listened.

Job stepped out of the cave to take in the night air and spend some time alone with the Spirit. As he left the inner light of the cave behind, he looked up, and thought he saw a silhouette cross one of the moons ... a silhouette that brought back memories.

"Father," he whispered. "Thank you. For all the days, for all the nights. For life that never ends."

He watched for the silhouette to pass again. It did not.

"For whatever adventure you send..."

Days passed. Gadol slept in the underground cavern, with dreams of savage acts towards the visitors filling his mind and delighting his heart. One particularly vivid dream prompted him to sudden flight, and he leapt into the air, immediately striking the ceiling of the cavern. He fell, awaking disoriented; his right wing slammed into a rock thrusting out from the cavern wall. As he struck the rock, he heard the crack of bone. Sudden pain stabbed up through the upper wing into his shoulder and back. He fell to the ground, half in the water, half on the gravel.

He attempted to move, and the pain gripped him without mercy. He lay absolutely still, and hours passed.

Untold time later, he awoke and tried to move. The pain surged in the wing, but it was duller and more diffused. Bearable, he thought. Slowly pushing up, he found ways to shift and turn that did not require that appendage to do anything it did not want to do.

Pulling himself into the water, he swam with other muscles, dragging the wing through the current, until he could float to the top. As he emerged in the rolling waves offshore he saw the figure of a man standing on the cliff above the cave.

Slipping beneath the surface, Gadol rested on the sea bottom for a few minutes, then slowly moved towards the shore. It should be dark within the hour, and he could emerge undetected. Hopefully.

But no more flying, not anytime soon. No communication with Tontal or others.

Food. Food would be difficult. Hunger already grumbled within him, and would become unbearable.

He reached the gravel beach and eased up onto the shoals. Exhausted from that effort, he slept again.

The wing ached. When he tried to lift it the pain was excruciating, and he finally gave up trying. Gadol huddled against the boulders and cliff face where the stream came plummeting down the cliff face and splashed out into the sea, drinking from the waterfall and easing into the waves to find food when he could. Days passed. The swelling finally went down, but the wing was useless.

Morning broke on the 6th day after the accident. Desperately hungry, Gadol clambered into the sea. Clumsily he moved into the deeper water, where he could move by body motion with no help from the wing.

Can't fly. Can't get where Tontal can hear me. Useless. Cursed planet.

His anger exploded, and great clouds of steam boiled up to the surface. Any fish that might have been near fled the heat, noise, and stink of his temper. Rolling over in the water, he floated to the surface like a dead thing, and let the waves gradually carry him back to the shore.

Rising to his feet, he dragged himself out of the foam and collapsed against the sheer wall beside the waterfall. Hungry, frustrated, and weak, he slept.

Job pointed him out.

"He's injured," he whispered to the others. "Has been struggling with it for a while. That right wing's useless."

We looked down at the dark grey body, apparently lifeless, crumpled against the cliff, lying partly under the waterfall. Splotches of mottled green and dark red wandered across his abdomen. Perhaps forty feet long, with great rough wings and heavily clawed feet, it would be a powerful animal when healthy.

"What is it?" I asked.

"One of Leviathan's brood," said Job. "Remember?"

"The sons of Pride," whispered Linus.

"Yes."

"I thought they were on Earth, or even extinct. How did he get here? Are there more?"

Job glanced at me before answering, then turned his gaze back to the wounded creature.

"Before the rebellion," he murmured, "they were beautiful. Mighty. But they joined Lucifer, in heart if not in action."

"They fought God?" I exclaimed. "This pitiful creature? I mean, he's big, but …"

"In heart, not in action," repeated Job. "And what you see is not what was. You can hardly imagine what he was, looking at him now."

"So, he's here as a prisoner," suggested John, "thrown down from a glorious life, and now trapped in a broken, physical body on a desolate planet."

The creature had not moved. If it were breathing, we couldn't tell from the distance.

"For how long?" asked Julia.

"Can't say how long he's been here. And how long he stays? Hmm. That may be up to him."

Job got to his feet. "Let's go." He began climbing down the rocks along the side of the waterfall.

"Where are you going?" exclaimed Julia.

"To meet him," smiled Job. "And to heal him, if he wants it!"

"And if God wants it, I suppose…" I said, and looked for a handhold. We scrambled down after him, not wanting to miss what was about to happen, no matter which way it went.

The animal stirred as he heard us coming, and looked up. When he saw us, he bolted to his feet and threw himself into the waves, disappearing immediately. Job kept going.

"Do you know his name?" I called down, grabbing for a less slippery rock to keep from falling.

"Not yet," replied Job, pausing to look up over his shoulder, "but I will soon, if I understand what Father has in mind!"

We worked our way down along the waterfall, careful step at a time, and stood on the narrow strand of gravel between the waves and the cliff, looking out over the water.

"He's there, watching us," said John. "I can feel him."

"Let's give him a few minutes," said Job.

We settled in on the rocks, and waited. No sound but the waves on the rocks, and the splashing of water falling behind us.

Job stood up and walked to the edge of the water. I stepped up next to him. In a quiet voice, he said, "Father, I don't think I should command him. Seems like it needs to be his choice. Will you bring him?" And waited.

Moments later, we saw the head rise from the water. The creature slowly walked towards us, his height becoming apparent as the water became more shallow and the massive body rose into sight.

"Spread out, give him room to settle down here on the gravel."

We backed up, and moved to each side. The beast came slowly, as though it were the last thing he would do of his own will. Finally standing before Job, looking down upon him, the thing stood without moving.

"Will you lie down? We mean you no harm."

A moment's pause, and it lowered its body to the ground, eyes fixed on Job.

"What is your name?"

Silence. Whether from not being able to speak, or not knowing how, I could not tell. I felt a violent struggle going on inside this creature, though he was outwardly calm.

"Livya … Livya-Gadol. Is that right?"

The huge head slowly dropped, and raised, and dropped again. Nodding. Still totally fixated on Job's face.

"Livya was the family name? Livya-than … Leviathan … is your father?"

"How did he know that?" I asked Julia. She shook her head. "A word of knowledge, I think. God told him. Or he's in communication with the thing, and it told him."

"Can it speak? Out loud? Something we would understand?"

"Must have been able to in the past, at least among its own kind. But now … in flesh … I guess we'll find out."

"Look at those wings!"

Job continued to hold the attention of the beast.

"We have dominion here," he said. "That is why God brought you to me, though I can tell that you would have avoided us if you could."

Gadol stared, a yellow flame burning in his eyes, his body now almost quivering with an obvious and barely restrained desire to get away.

"Your wing is broken."

Silence.

"Would you like it healed?"

The animal turned its head, as though hearing something he could not understand, and stared intently at Job.

"You can do this?" The voice was rough, but clear, and obviously struggling with incomprehension. I stared, fascinated.

"I can ask the One, and he can do it."

Gadol snorted, and began to turn away. He shook violently, as though a fever raged within him. Maybe it did, but a fever not of sickness.

"Gadol." Job called him back to full attention, gently and firmly.

"Would you like it to be healed?"

A long silence followed. He stared at Job, and quivered.

"Something he desperately wants, being offered by someone he hates, through someone he despises, is my guess," whispered John.

In the end he accepted.

"Being crippled is apparently worse than being helped."

"Barely!"

Gadol eased his head down before Job's feet, rage and desperation and revulsion swirling in his mind and heart, steeling himself to stay, to stay just long enough, just … until … the touch of … this man.

Job, of all people. Job!

How they had relished Lucifer's treatment of him. He amazed them by his response. He stayed loyal, even to the One who let all that happen, even after all that! Why?

And now. To meet here, and like this.

And to accept … worse, to need … kindness and sympathy from him.

And to be waiting for, desperately hoping for a touch of healing from the One he reviled, the One for whom his heart had nothing but bitterness. The One he hated beyond all measure.

He shook violently, and forced himself still.

Job reached up to place a hand on the ridge above Gadol's eyes that ran up and over the scales of his head and down his back.

"Let him know You," he murmured after a minute or so.

Then he moved around to Gadol's side, stepping into the surf where the damaged wing hung awkwardly into the water. Placing a hand over the broken bone, where the wing took an unexpected turn and the end of a snapped bone protruded from the heavy skin, he closed his eyes and slowly turned his face to the sky.

"He's going to heal *that*?" I marveled.

"If you had more time, you could just stay and watch!"

"That's a great idea. Thanks, Julia, I think I will. Don't really have to be anywhere for … oh, millennia!"

We laughed, and quickly sobered as we watched Job stand quietly over the beast.

He looked up at us. "You could pray too," he suggested. "It's not like I've ever done this before!"

He stood with a hand on the shattered wing for the longest time. Finally, he spoke. "Be healed."

I didn't quite see what happened. The beast shook himself, stood, and brought both wings up over his body, extending them fully. Then he simply leapt into the air, and using his wings as I would use my hands to climb a ladder, he climbed. In seconds, he was a speck in the sky, and then he was gone.

Gadol climbed and climbed, desperate to be away from the people, and exulting in being in the air again. Higher and higher, unmindful of his weary and spent condition, he reached for the depths of the universe, or as close as he could get.

"Tontal!" he cried out, as the air grew cold and thin, and the stars were plainly visible above him. "Job is here! They are beginning. The planet is green!"

Silence. He pushed higher, straining, suddenly realizing he had no reserves at all, and would fall within moments. Exhausted, he coasted, gliding, waiting.

"Join them," came the answer. "Befriend them. Get them to trust you."

"No!" shouted Gadol, with all the revulsion he felt for these that God had sent. "How can we … what are you …" His voice failed him, in his confusion.

After a moment, as Gadol began falling towards the clouds far below, the answer came back.

"Then we will destroy them."

Seven

A week later Gadol was back. A changed creature, apparently grateful for what Job had done. We were camping in the open fields several miles from the cave, about to explore a valley that seemed to extend for miles, a deep ravine connecting the mountains we had seen across the desert … what used to be desert … and the sea.

He coasted in circles around our camp, drifting down from well above the clouds, and landed a few yards away. Job stood and walked towards him a few steps. We all stood. I was wondering what would come of this.

"You have returned," Job observed.

"Yes."

A moment of silence. Gadol seemed to be gathering his thoughts. "Thank you."

"You're welcome, Gadol. Is it better? Is the pain gone?"

"Yes."

More silence.

"Is there something else we can do for you?"

"No. But I might be able to … to help you." He shook for a moment, or quivered. His whole body trembled. Then he focused again on Job. "What are you … doing?"

Job turned to us, and raised his eyebrows, asking if he should proceed. We were obviously hesitant. He turned back to Gadol.

"Let us consider that. Could we talk again later?"

Gadol nodded, and seemed to just step up into the air, the powerful wings lifting his great grey body effortlessly, revealing the splotches of mottled green and dark red across his abdomen.

Job returned to his seat, and we gathered around, returning to our mid-day meal.

"I don't think so!" said John.

"Why not?" asked Julia. "He could fly us around! We could map out the planet so much faster with his help! We could really see what's here!"

Job nodded.

"And we have so little time to get it done," I added, giving Julia my most serious look. She looked at the sky and groaned.

"Seems to have had a major change of heart," said John. "He could hardly stand to have you touch him, before. Talk to us, Job. What do think is going on?" John fixed his gaze on Job, and waited.

Job leaned back and pulled a few more grapes off the cluster in his hand. He looked around without speaking.

"I'm OK with it," said Linus. "God's with us, we have dominion here, and he's obviously going to be here with us. Let's see if we can work with him."

"What's your thought?" asked Job, turning to me.

I rubbed my face. "Worries me. People don't change that quickly, but I don't know about … whatever he is. Seems unlikely, though. That look in his eyes when you healed him was not pretty. How long will he be here, do you know?"

Job sighed. "I think Father is waiting for him to decide where his allegiance lies. So it depends on him. Maybe this is a first step towards reconciliation."

I chewed on that.

"It's the Father's way," continued Job, "to offer repentance and healing. We think of his sacrifice as having removed our sin, and don't think much about the effect of that on the rest of the universe, other creatures, etc. But do you remember the scripture about the creation waiting in travail for the sons of God to be revealed?"

I did.

"He's part of creation. Long before man, actually."

That was how Gadol became part of the team. Next time he came, Job talked with him, and agreed to work with him. I'm sure he was lonely, before we came, but I'm also sure we weren't exactly the company he wanted to keep. An uneasy alliance, it seemed to me. But Julia liked him, and Linus and Job seemed to be comfortable. John did not like it, and Gadol soon picked up on that. I couldn't tell what was going on, so, as always, I left it before God and waited.

Tontal began reaching out to others of the Dominant, now that he had found Gadol. Soon he had located Livya-Ruunt, perhaps the least intelligent of the brood, and Livya-Guntel, the one he could most easily control.

But knowing where they were was not enough.

For a long time, an idea had been forming in his mind. They still had some shred of their earlier abilities, from being spirit. They could still communicate, in a limited, difficult fashion.

Could they travel? Could they also use the slipstreams between the stars to bypass physical space, to move through the universe at will, as they once did?

Gathering them all to one place was the next step.

Could he work with 'Athaq to do this? 'Athaq ruled the star where Gadol was held, and certainly the Watchers made use of the slipstreams.

He considered that for a long time before discarding the idea. 'Athaq was untrustworthy, and would reveal them as likely as not. He wanted to use 'Athaq, not be at risk because of him.

Was 'Athaq one of those? One of those 'sons of God' that mated with human women, producing the Nephilim? Probably not, or he wouldn't have dominion in Alnitak. But maybe. Certainly something he could be accused of, if that were useful.

Eventually he decided to use Ruunt for the experiment, rather than risk his own life. Ruunt would do what he was told, eventually, and would be the least loss if he didn't survive the trip.

Moving into the upper atmosphere, he called out.

"Ruunt!"

He coasted for a time, conserving energy. The effort to stay this high was significant, so this would be a short conversation.

"Ruunt!"

Ruunt was on 'Athnon, near Saiph, nearly 200 light-years away, but over the solar connection that distance would not matter much. If he were awake, Ruunt would begin climbing into the sky upon hearing his name, and it would take a few minutes for him to respond.

Tontal climbed higher, to allow gliding while in communication, and still be high enough that this would work. His lungs burned with the lack of sufficient oxygen. The mountains where he lived were specks among the clouds far below. Stars blazed around him, it seemed, as he flew in the midnight sky.

Finally Ruunt responded.

"I want you to come here."

"How?" came the reply.

"Use the slipstreams. When you come past this planet, I'll pull you in."

Silence. Ruunt obviously could guess the risk as well as Tontal.

"When?"

"Twenty-six hours. It'll be lined up then. I'm between you and Mintaka. Tell me before you do it."

"Why me?"

He always resists, thought Tontal. Has to have everything explained. Better to just flatter him.

"I need you here, so we can work out how to get the others."

More silence. Tontal's patience wore away.

"Why can't you come here?" came the reply from Ruunt.

"I've got four stars to pull you here. Mintaka, remember? You've just got Saiph. And we need to move you this way anyway. Twenty-six hours from now."

Tontal dropped toward the planet's surface. Better to leave it at that, and not extend the discussion. He would do it. Or regret it.

Job was ready to call forth some animal life, now that the seas were teeming and 'Nsol had become a green, fertile place. Lush grasses covered the land in all directions, and the wind, cooler now, no longer brought dust and sand into our faces. Trees were growing rapidly on the hillsides and up the mountains. If seasons were to come, this was certainly spring or summer.

The desert we had arrived in was now a wide, beautiful plain stretching between the coastal cliffs and the mountains that had been on our left that day. Those mountains had been calling us, blue in the distance with snow on the peaks and covered in what might be pine and fir. I wanted to see them from the air, and have some idea what was behind them. I offered to be the first of Gadol's passengers, since I used to love flying and none of the others would have had that experience.

After staring at me for a long minute, Gadol agreed. Did I smell bad? Was it a step across a line he really did not want to cross? I couldn't tell. He turned his side to me, and extended a wing and shoulder towards the ground. I grabbed hold of the rough, heavy skin, and found it to be surprisingly cold, and a little damp. I expected hot, dry flesh, but it was not. He cringed a little at my touch, I think, but we both adjusted quickly. I tried to crawl up on hands and knees, not to step on him with my boots, but I had to get a foothold to get up onto his back.

The ridge down his back was not something you could sit on.

"Job, I can't settle in here. Have we got something to make a seat, a saddle?"

Job unpacked a bed pallet and some cord, and tossed them up to me. The pallet was amazing. It smoothed out the jagged edges of the beast's ridged back just like it smoothed out the rocks of the cave floor. I rolled it up into a flattened bundle, set it between two of the bigger spikes just behind his neck, and tied it to them so it wouldn't shift around. I settled down on it, and decided things weren't going to get any better.

"I'm ready, I guess."

I swallowed hard, and the beast convulsed his powerful muscles and leapt up. I suddenly realized my feet were in the way of his wings, and pulled them up behind me. Given a choice of my being comfortable or his having full use of the wings, there was no choice. I certainly wasn't going to ask him to change anything.

What looked effortless from the ground was obviously hard work on his part. He must have weighed several tons, but it was all muscle, which was not entirely a comforting thought.

He veered towards the mountains. We began climbing just above the trees, gliding around the ridges and following the ravines and gorges to ascend more easily. We crossed back and forth over one particular ravine where waterfall after waterfall testified to the rapidly changing elevation. As yet, there were no animals or birds in those forests, no beetles or snakes or foxes, no bats nor the insects for them to chase, but all that would come. It was totally uninhabited, but majestic, nonetheless.

We crested a ridge and the view was breathtaking. The mountain sloped down before me into a deep, wooded valley. On the other side a higher range rose up, this time climbing far above the timber line to show raw granite topping out into vast smooth boulders and shelves, then up again to snow-lined crevices and high, frozen peaks.

"Can you breathe?" roared Gadol, and I realized I was doing fine, even at several thousand feet above the plains. Other than clinging to his back in a state bordering on terror, that is.

"Yes!" I shouted back.

He suddenly veered, in response. Straight up. I clung to the cords and closed my eyes.

After a few moments he leveled off, and began a wide, sweeping circle back over the range we had just passed. In a few minutes I saw the plains I had stood on just a short time before, and realized my friends must be there watching. Could they see me? I could certainly not pick them out!

But from this height, I could see the geography underneath Gadol's wings much more clearly. Maybe that was his purpose.

When we finished a wide circle and headed back toward the snow-covered peaks, I realized he had also been climbing. We were now even with those peaks, and I looked down into a valley running for many miles between two mountain ranges.

And beyond those highest peaks, I could see further ranges, at least as high.

In the valley below us, I noticed a lake. Having no idea of the scale of things down there, I guessed it to be three or four miles long and a mile wide, and it seemed to be the source of the stream that ran across the lower valley and past our cave into the sea.

"Let's go there," I shouted, pointing at it. He glanced back to see where I pointed, and folded his wings. We plummeted. Since he was pointed straight down, there was nothing between my face and that lake but thousands of feet of … nothing. I don't think I screamed, but, honestly, I don't know.

We seemed seconds away from plunging into the deep blue, beautiful waters, when he spread his wings and leveled off, the force of the turn driving me into his back. I'm surprised I don't still have the new shape I took on, from that pressure and his spiked backbone driving itself into my body at that moment.

When I was able to open my eyes, we were skimming the lake, barely above its surface. I could see all the way to the bottom, it was so clear, and I think it was not shallow. Nothing moved in it, of course, but our reflection and that of the few, high clouds we had just left behind.

Gadol dipped a claw into it, throwing a high stream into the air and splashing it on me. Icy cold it was, and he knew it. Felt good to both of us, perhaps.

We were still moving incredibly fast, and the far shore came roaring at us. He swept up over the tops of the nearest trees, and circled around. At the far side, the north, I think, there was a waterfall feeding the lake from higher sources, and on the southern end an even longer waterfall dropped down a thousand feet or more of sheer rock walls to the foothills and on into the valley.

Gadol swept up over the front range and began a long, slow glide down the front of that slope, sweeping far to the north, then circling out over the plains and flying far to the south. Another stream flowed out of the woods several miles to the south, and seemed to flow south from that point, where ours ran almost due west until it plummeted into the sea.

Finally we soared down to the plains, and the last few miles back to the team he flew so close to the ground I could have picked flowers as we passed them.

"Are you holding on?" he roared.

What kind of a question was that? I gripped tightly, suddenly not at all sure I wanted to find out what he had in mind. As we approached the camp where Job and the others had a fire going, he turned straight up for about a quarter mile, then did a barrel role or two, and flipped head over tail, before plunging straight down. Just before hitting the ground, he flipped his feet under him and landed, like a gymnast coming off the high bar and sticking it to the mat. Again, the ridges and spikes rammed into my body, but the pallet cushioned it amazingly well.

And there we were, standing still, everyone watching, waiting for me to get down.

Right.

I slowly unfolded myself, lifting up from the desperation position to the flight enjoyment position, and then slowly lifting my right foot out of the cramped position it had been in for what seemed like hours. I tried to extend it. I tried again. I decided to try the left one.

Gadol quivered, and I had the distinct impression he was ready for the experience to end.

I pushed my left foot out straight, then went back to the right one. It was finally ready to be used again. Untying the cords, I tossed them and the pallet down to Linus, then swung a leg over the spine and slid down to the ground.

Where I fell down.

Julia rushed to me and gave me a hand to pull up with. I stood, shaking a little, getting my land legs back under me.

"Well?" Seems like they all spoke at once.

I turned to Gadol. "Thank you," I said, and he looked at me for a moment. He then moved away, and casually launched into a slow, horizontal glide towards the sea. To wash off? Maybe just for dinner. We had been up there a while.

"What did you see?" asked Job, as we walked over to the fire. Night was falling now, and the stars peeked out through the dusky blue. I kept being surprised to look up and see patterns of stars totally different than the ones I grew up under.

"I can't tell you how beautiful it is!" I said, suddenly sitting down. "Excuse me. Legs are a little shaky!"

They laughed, and settled down around the fire.

"Beyond this range, there's another, even higher, with snow on top. And beyond that, even more, maybe higher. And just over this one, a long lake, the water so clear and blue you can't believe it. And cold!"

"How do you know that?" asked John. "You were up in the air."

"Did you see how we came back, flying low over the ground?"

"Yes. What was he doing?"

"I don't know, but he seems to like doing that. We flew over the lake that low, and he soaked me!"

"Any life, anywhere?" asked Linus.

"None that I saw. I think that part is up to us, right, Job?"

He nodded. "Whenever you're ready, I am!"

Ruunt coasted back down from the edges of space, down towards the southern continent, down through the cold black clouds of the raging thunderstorm below him. The tingle of the electrical charges felt good, and he had no thought of the lightning doing him harm. The violent winds threw him down faster, then suddenly sideways. When they started lifting him up again, he turned down and broke out into the rain below.

Why did Tontal want him? He chewed on his tongue, forgetting the lesson learned yesterday, and the day before.

His island appeared through the sheets of rain, starkly outlined by a moon lazing on the horizon. He coasted over the first ridge and dropped into the lake that washed its slopes. Relaxing completely, he floated slowly back to the surface and drifted there, pummeled by the storm and hidden in the darkness.

Tontal was a bully. Why couldn't he just leave everyone alone?

Ruunt sulked, until he grew tired of sulking. Turning over, he slipped under the waves and moved toward shore, undulating like an eel. Coming to the gravel shore, he climbed up and wandered towards the overhanging cliffs. The carcass of the last boar he had eaten still lay at the edge of the lake where he cast it aside. Suddenly hungry from the effort of flying so high, he settled down to gnaw at the raw meat for a time.

The storm was easing and stars began filling the sky under its eastern edge as he finally trundled under cover of the rock above, out of the remaining drizzle.

Well, why not? Why not give it a try? Nothing to stay here for. No life, except for those wretched pigs. Those mean, ugly, wretched pigs. Of all things to eat, why did the One give him that? No fish, no birds, not even a weed; just the pigs, day after endless day.

But the slipstreams, what would that be like? Bound in flesh, could he even do it? Was Tontal using him as the test since he was the smallest one, the one that didn't matter?

His hatred of Tontal inflamed his suspicions, and he hated him more. Just because he was smallest, and not as quick as the others to know what was going on. Just because they were so sure of themselves, all of them. Just because …

His bitter imagination carried him into fitful sleep, and he woke with the late morning sun glaring at him over the lake.

Looking at the barren rock, the empty water, and his next meal slopping up water on the other side, he decided. Whatever was there could not be worse than staying here. Surely.

Eight

We looked at each other. "Things won't be as quiet around here, you know that!" said John. "We're going to be a lot busier!"

"And, you wanted … more time on the beach?" asked Julia.

'That's what I want, for sure!" said Linus. "In fact, any time on the beach, anywhere, would be interesting! That bit of sand in front of the cave is the closest I've ever been, and I'm tired of just hearing about it!"

"Didn't see any beach around that lake. Sorry!" I reported. "But when we see some more of the shoreline of that ocean, we'll find some for you. We have no idea how big that piece of water is… could be islands out there, who knows what!"

"Back to the question?" Job said. "Are we ready to populate this place?"

"Let's do it," I said. "But wait …'

They looked at me.

"Will they be wild? Dangerous? Or is this when the lion and the lamb like each other?"

Job laughed. "The wildness on Earth came with sin, remember?"

"Yes …"

"He took care of that. It's done. Now … the real issue is the freedom he gives all of his creation to make choices. Even the trees, even the angels, even … you and me. Even Gadol."

I studied on this for a minute. Several, actually. What would be the effect of Adam's sin on this planet? How did the Cross change that? What would be the condition of new breeds of animals, brought forth on new planets, after the atonement on Earth?

"Have you thought this through, Job? Do you know?"

"No. I've tried. I think we have yet another mystery on our hands, and we just need to take the adventure as it comes, led by Him. Just like we always do."

"Are we through talking yet?" asked Linus. "I'm ready to see what He does!"

"All right," said Job. "First thing in the morning."

"What?" I blurted out. But he was already rolling out his pallet and stretching out, looking at the stars.

"What about that one," he said, pointing to four stars that formed a long rectangle, and a smaller set near them that suggested a small box or stool. "Let's call that one 'the Throne' -- what do you think?"

I liked it.

When the pink light of morning flooded over us, casting the shadows of the mountain range far out into the valley, we were already up.

"Let's do it!" said Julia. "John has never seen a parrot, or an eagle, or a lion or a bear. Or even a rabbit! Let's show him some things!"

"Do I have to guess their names, or will you tell me?" he laughed.

"Well, Adam got to name everything," Job retorted. "You want to name some things?"

"Sure," said John. "The first thing I see, we'll call 'Julia'!"

"OK, Job, give us something interesting to be called a 'Julia'," I said.

Job was quiet. After a moment he said, "I think we simply ask Father to bring it forth, just like we did the plants and the sea creatures. I don't think we get to choose!"

He stepped out of the camp and faced the woods and the rising slopes.

"Father, I think we're ready, and this is as good a place as any. Shall I do it?"

After a moment he raised his hand towards the trees and said, as quietly and simply as could be, "Come forth."

For a few moments, the same stillness reigned that we had become accustomed to. Then a low, distant moan started, high up on the ridge. It rose in volume and pitch, until it reminded me of the howl of a coyote over the night plains in South Dakota.

"That's not a good sign," I muttered.

John looked at me, his expression unreadable. I decided he was amused, not worried. I looked back at the hills, a little less eager for what was to come, trying to remind myself that things were very, very different now. And here.

A squeal broke through the silence, then a deep, long roar, then all sorts of chittering, chirps, and barks, and a vast symphony of new life erupted with every imaginable kind of sound.

I felt something touch my ankle, and looked down to see a Buttermilk Racer curling up around my foot. With an effort, I held still. Several feet away a small white rabbit sat staring at me, head cocked. Two brown field mice scampered past him, and a mole tunnel began appearing in the soil in front of John, who watched it in fascination.

"What is it?" he asked, glancing up. "It looks like a mouse," I replied, "but with long, sharp front claws and the ability to go through the earth like Gadol goes through the air!"

He stared at the tunnel, then suddenly dug his hand deep into the soft soil just in front of the tunnel-maker. Nothing happened. The tunnel stopped where his hand had gone in. He slowly raised his hand, and in his palm stood a light grey mole, waiting, completely unafraid.

"On Earth, they don't see very well. Bring it close to your face, so he can focus on you."

John raised his hand, bringing the mole within inches of his eyes. It sat up, cocked its head, and stared at him.

"Your claws really are made for digging, aren't they!" exclaimed John. He inspected the little creature. It settled down in his hand and simply waited, apparently content and without fear.

"I don't think this is a 'Julia'," he laughed. "Looks more like a Sam!" He set the mole back into the hole, and it promptly disappeared. A new tunnel appeared.

When I looked back toward the forest I saw a vast parade of animals and birds emerging, a crowd beyond numbering. They walked and flew out from the trees and underbrush, or appeared in the branches of the nearest trees. They came towards us as though coming to water on a hot day, as though they knew us and were coming to be greeted. Gathering around us and coming together into groups of like creatures, they sat or perched or lay on the grass, rank upon rank, apparently comfortable with each other and with us. Birds settled on shoulders and backs and tails, and their hosts did not object. Smaller animals lay against larger animals as though they were old friends. The view amazed me as I remembered the way of the food chain on earth.

"Welcome," said Job. A murmur of growls and yaps and chirps and hoots moved across the crowd, and they were still again.

"All that you see is yours. Father welcomes you to life, and to your home, and so do we. Enjoy the good things of the land. Spread out and occupy this world. Come to us if you have need, and we will do what we can to help you."

"What else should we tell them?" he asked, turning to us.

Facing them again, he described the country around us, to give them each a sense of where they might find territory to their liking, from the seacoast to the high mountain slopes. He then introduced each of us to the assembly, as though completely confident that they understood him and would remember our names.

When he finished, Job dismissed them, and together they rose. Each of them drifted off into the woods or out onto the plains, or up into the air, to seek a home. In moments we stood alone again, but the world now vibrated with a completely new undercurrent of sound and life.

We spent the rest of the day working our way up the front face of the nearest range. The large sun had just touched the horizon behind us when Julia and I reached the top of the cliffs, came over the edge, and stood up on the plateau.

"Oh," said Julia. I looked around. A tall man in blue and white robes stood there as though he had been waiting for us to come up from the valley.

There was something unusual about him, something that invited you to peace and contentment. He nodded, but did not speak. We stood silently and waited for the others to arrive. Who could this be? No other men were here, as far as I knew.

The others slowly emerged from the climb. John and Linus saw us and the stranger, and came to our side. Job was the last one up.

"My old friend!" he exclaimed, tossing aside his backpack and striding up to greet the stranger. "What a pleasure to see you, and what a surprise!" They embraced, and Job turned to the rest of us.

"You have not met? This is Melchizedek, King of Salem, priest of God forever, with no beginning and no end."

The team stepped forward one at a time to be introduced, and then he looked us over. "How good it is to see the first of Adam's sons move out into the Universe, finally taking their place."

"I thought only Jesus was "the beginning and the end," I said. "How can you, a man like us, be alive without having had a mother or father, and be a priest "because of an indestructible life" -- isn't that what the scripture said? -- before Jesus cut the new covenant on the cross?"

Melchizedek laughed. "He goes right to the core, doesn't he?"

"Usually!" Job nodded. "Come, everyone, sit down, it was a long climb and I could use the rest." We gathered where Melchizedek had spread a blanket over the soft grass. He offered a bowl of grapes and figs from a great woven bag sitting there, and as we passed them around, he settled down onto the blanket with us.

He looked at me, smiling. "I'll give you the same opportunity that Jesus gave those priests and teachers," he said. "If you'll answer my question, I'll answer yours."

"All right," I said, after hesitating a moment.

"Tell me," said Melchizedek, "am I really a man like yourself?"

I stared at him. The scripture had not said he was. In fact, the implication of his not having mother or father, or beginning or end, was that he clearly was not a man like us.

I looked around. Job was smiling, but the others were looking intently at Melchizedek. He sat before us, looking very much as any man might look. He ate fruit as a man would. Yet when Abraham met him after that famous battle, he was already ancient, and known as a priest of the God whom Abraham followed. As far as Abraham had known, no one else in the world even knew this God who was leading him ... except Melchizedek.

"I ... don't know!"

Melchizedek laughed again, and the joy of the Father was evident in every wrinkle of his face. He winked at me, then turned to face Job more directly.

"How are you doing in the work before you, my friend?"

"It goes well." Job looked around for the team to agree, or not. Everyone nodded.

"The world flourishes, the seas are alive, and the creatures of the woods and plains are finding their way."

Melchizedek nodded, listening, waiting.

"One of Leviathan's kin is here," Job continued. "He's offered to help us."

Melchizedek nodded.

"Should I trust him?"

The One offers forgiveness to all who repent," murmured Melchizedek. "Perhaps he will. Perhaps he has."

"I think not," said John, "but I am the only one."

Melchizedek smiled at him. "Let your Father show you. Now as always, the Spirit leads us into all truth."

John smiled back. "'Your' Father, did you say? Not ... 'our' Father?"

Everyone laughed. "You'll catch me yet, won't you?" said Melchizedek. "I'll let you worry it a bit. Give you something to mull over, out on the prairies!"

He looked around. "Tell me ... what's your favorite part of the new creation, so far?"

Julia spoke first. "A butterfly as big as my hand!" she exclaimed. "With more shades of blue and green and purple in its wings than I've ever seen!"

"Linus?"

"The big bears, and the lions, the cats. There's a peace in them that's amazing. They're content!"

"I saw that in the serpents, too," I added. "That's what seemed so different about them! They're not skittish, not afraid or belligerent!"

"I've never seen them behave any other way," said John, thoughtfully, without a hint of a smile. "I never met a snake in my entire life that ... never mind."

"But you've never ... humph!" Julie pushed him over.

We explained the joke to Melchizedek, and he laughed. "Well, then. That's settled!"

"Tell us about Abraham," I asked. "Did you know him, before he came back from that battle with all those kings, when he gave you a tenth of all they had taken?"

"I knew of him. He knew of me. As far as I recall, we had not met."

"You knew God, even then."

"Of course."

"And he had left everything to follow a God no one else knew … just a voice he heard, that even his wife did not hear. They must have thought he was insane."

"Yes." He smiled. "Yes, actually, they did."

"Was there anyone else who knew God … who didn't just worship the idols … besides you and him?"

"Not many, then. Not many."

"I've never thought about this before, but … how is it you met that day?"

"I sought him out. I heard he had passed that way, and would be coming back -- assuming they were successful, of course -- so I was looking for him."

"Why?"

The others were listening intently, so I did not feel badly about being the only one talking. Job seemed amused, and I guess he enjoyed watching me stumble about in these conversations!

"As you say, few knew the One. His glory was plain to see in the world around us, and how men could think those stone and wood things were something you could worship -- well, I never understood that level of blindness!"

He pulled a few more grapes off the cluster, and was quiet for a moment.

"Did you ever have the experience," he asked, looking up at me, "of being in worship before the Throne, and being aware of others who were also there in the spirit?"

"Yes … I think so. Sometimes I would have the feeling that a certain person must also be in worship at the same time. Is that what you mean?"

"Exactly," he smiled. "When I turned to God, I was often aware of another who was doing the same. It was Abram … or, Abraham, as God named him after the blood covenant, after the promises were made. So I sought him, this fellow worshipper, to share a meal and to know his face. I wanted to sit with him, to know him."

"What was he like, then?"

At the appointed time, Ruunt flew reluctantly into the upper atmosphere. How would this work, in a straining body of flesh and tired muscle? He rose above all clouds, above all interference. He remembered using these paths when they were spirit … only spirit … not in these pitiful physical bodies. The glittering streams that flowed among the stars. The highways of heaven. The music streaming through the galaxies, the colors exploding from the stars that no physical eye could see. The dance of …

Lack of oxygen brought him back to where he was. Searing pain ran through his chest, straining muscles screamed for relief, and his vision began to fail. Now or never, he thought. I'm not going back, if I can help it.

He focused his mind on the stream he knew was there, all around him. Using them had been so automatic, it was hard to remember what actually happened, how you entered and left them.

He turned toward the star Mintaka, unmistakable over the eastern horizon of 'Athnon. Reaching out to what he could not see, but thought he could sense, he willed himself into it.

For a moment, nothing happened, and he felt himself near to blacking out.

"Now!" he screamed in his mind, and with whatever will and strength he had left, he threw himself towards Mintaka.

Color exploded in his head, brilliant streams of light swirled around him, and the agony of the moment before was swallowed up in terror and unbelievable pain. Stars that had been his roadmap a moment before blurred into streaks of white light that crossed the entire universe.

What … have … I … done …?

Nine

Tontal felt him coming, as he hovered in the thin air, reaching out in his mind to sense the streams, to sense the traffic on them. How would he know when Ruunt came?

He realized suddenly that it should not be difficult; the creature would be the first physical thing ever to travel those slipstreams, and if he survived, would be as obvious as a fire in the night.

If he did it when I told him to …

Tontal could feel his own strength failing, trying to stay this high with so little air for his wings to catch. Peering away from Mintaka into the blackness of empty space, anything physical should be quite visible, lit up by the star behind him.

Then he saw Ruunt, whether with his physical eyes or just in his spirit, he could not tell. The black object would be past in an instant, hurtling into the star it was aimed at, if not diverted. Suddenly he had the same confusion Ruunt had wrestled: how does a physical being interact with traffic on the slipstreams?

He realized it shouldn't matter; he and Ruunt were physical, regardless of the stream that carried him.

He would have one chance to reach Ruunt physically; the slipstream flowed around the planet and its atmosphere without slowing, as a river flows past a boulder. But just a slight diversion… He reached out in his mind, with his will, in his spirit, physically, he knew not, and tried to pull Ruunt down as he reached 'Nsela. Ruunt slipped to the edge of the stream, then tumbled out of it, but sped past Tontal at incredible speed. Tontal could only watch, and then Ruunt was gone.

He began coasting down. Stars filled the sky, and the sense of the slipstream was lost to him.

Suddenly he saw Ruunt again: he was orbiting the planet! Tontal thrust himself higher, and tried to accelerate in the direction Ruunt was hurtling, but could not reach his path before he was past.

"One more chance…" he thought, and pushed higher. "He'll be lower next time."

Minutes later, Ruunt approached again, and Tontal got close enough to get a claw on him. Ruunt's momentum jerked him forward, but Tontal's added mass changed their path and they fell together, tumbling into the lower atmosphere.

Eventually they slowed, as Tontal spread his wings to catch the thickening air. For a moment he let go of Ruunt, and shifted to a better grip. Then he realized how bruised and burnt the smaller animal was, and that he was quite unconscious. He carried Ruunt below him, wondering if were alive or dead.

They coasted down to the sea, and Tontal flew low enough to splash Ruunt through the waves, trying to wake him. There was no reaction. He rose to the cliff top and coasted to the ground, dropping the smaller creature onto the dirt and gravel near the opening to his cave. Without looking further at him, Tontal collapsed to the ground as well, exhausted.

When he woke some hours later, Ruunt was moaning and moving slightly. Tontal pushed on him with a claw.

"Wake up!"

Ruunt's eyes opened, staring without seeing. Slowly they focused, and recognition woke in his gaze.

"Tontal?"

Tontal did not answer. He turned, and moved to his shallow pool to refresh himself while Ruunt came to his senses.

"Tontal? How did you …"

"Never mind. How did you get into the stream?"

"I … don't know. It was there, I couldn't see it … there was nothing else to do, I just pushed into it."

"What did it feel like?"

Ruunt stared at him. Tontal saw in his eyes the excruciating pain of the acceleration and crushing force he had endured, the pain Ruunt could not put into words.

"We have to do it again."

Ruunt moaned, and Tontal began to wonder about his plan. Would his experience be worse, being bigger? Would he survive?

'Athnon stood in the valley where Ruunt had lived, considering the matter. Ruunt was gone, obviously. A pig squirmed deeper into the mud at the edge of the lake in front of Ruunt's cave. Another slept at the opening, where he would have been devoured if Ruunt were here.

He thought of the star Saiph, and moved towards it, his departure plunging the cave and lake back into the midnight darkness in which he had found it. The deep cold of space affected him no more than the blistering inferno of the star's core, and he settled into the heart of the star by long habit. This would bear some thought.

It may be that 'Athaq could help, he thought. Gadol was a problem, and 'Athaq had been trying to create a relationship with him, coax the creature towards repentance. A visit would be appropriate.

He drifted slowly from the star's core to its surface, enjoying every layer, moving from the swirl of nuclear fire at the center to the shooting flames of the outer corona as they leapt hundreds of miles into space. He left the star behind for the frozen vacuum that surrounded it and moved along the lightstream, considering.

Ruunt was gone. There was no way for him to leave, in his body of flesh, yet he had. Leviathan's brood knew the slipstreams, of course, but 'Athnon knew of no physical being that had ever attempted their use. Of course, no physical being even knew they existed. Until now.

He approached Alnitak, the triple star that was 'Athaq's home, and spoke. 'Athaq came to the surface of the blue giant, his brilliance surrounded by swirls of molten metal streaming in pure reds and golds, and awaited him there.

"Welcome, 'Athnon. May I serve you in some way?"

"Blessing to you, 'Athaq, and the peace of the One."

"The peace of the One," replied 'Athaq in the usual form.

"Ruunt appears to have left 'Nsial, and even the region of Saiph," 'Athnon continued. "I know of only one way that could have happened, yet I cannot understand how he would have done it."

"He is not there? You are certain?"

"The planet is empty, except the swine provided for his food. I would know if he were there, of course."

"Of course," said 'Athaq.

They considered things for a moment.

"The slipstream would destroy him, even if he could enter it … access it somehow in his fleshly state …" mused 'Athnon. "To him it would be light, nothing more."

"Thank you, 'Athnon. Let me consider it for a time."

"Of course. Blessings."

'Athaq stood for a bit after 'Athnon left. A mile-wide stream of liquid fire burst past him, reaching out for the stars. As it reached the height its energy allowed, the pulsing flame fell back in all directions, back into the molten ocean around him.

"I wonder," mused 'Athaq. "I wonder. Is he here?"

Turning his mind to the planet 'Nsol, 'Athaq disappeared from the surface of Alnitak. Moments later, he stood on a high ridge overlooking the coastline of 'Nsol, his brilliance washing out the pale early morning light. Nothing stirred in the vegetation that covered the cliffside between him and the surf.

A small, dark shape appeared far above, and Gadol drifted down from the cloudless sky in wide circles. From any distance, Gadol would see him standing here, and come. 'Athaq waited.

Gadol slowly descended. He landed some distance away and crouched warily, looking at his unwelcome visitor and offering no greeting.

'Athaq stood motionless, waiting.

"You wanted something, Watcher?"

"Have you met the team that has come with Job?"

"They are wandering the planet. I carry them, sometimes, to see from above."

"Really! They asked you to do that?"

"I offered."

'Athaq smiled, and wondered what his motivation could have been.

"Has anyone else come?"

No answer.

'Athaq waited.

"You are thinking of someone?" asked the huge creature, quietly.

"Ruunt comes to mind, for some reason."

"No. He is not here."

Gadol raised a back claw, and pressed into the muscle above the right wing. After a moment, he relaxed again, and looked back at 'Athaq.

"Is he gone from wherever the One put him?"

"Apparently."

"I would be interested in knowing how he left."

"So would I, Gadol. So would I. Is there anyone you could ask?"

Gadol sneered. "I suppose so. I think I will."

"Thank you."

'Athaq was suddenly gone.

Gadol stretched and relaxed, letting his eyes adjust to the normal light.

"I suppose that means he wants an answer…"

Job stepped out of the cave, the morning light just seeping into the sky and making the wide sweep of valley visible. A brilliant light suddenly illuminated everything surrounding him, and he turned to face it. A man stood there, or something very like a man, but made of liquid fire and much taller.

"Welcome," said Job. "Your name?"

The sun-man bowed. "I am 'Athaq. You are within my domain." He motioned to the massive sun glimmering on the horizon, about to burst into full light. "That is my home. And it is I who should welcome you, for the One has sent you."

"I am Job, come with my friends to shepherd this planet into life."

"I see what you have done. And yes, Job, I know you. I stood with the

One when Lucifer came to sift you. We watched your life unfold under his cruelty, and the blessing that came after, the blessing of your Father. You stood, in that trial. It astounded us all."

"The cloud of witnesses was larger than I thought!" exclaimed Job.

'Athaq stood without speaking for a few moments, and Job waited.

"I am concerned about Gadol," the Watcher finally said.

Job nodded.

"Have you found him helpful?"

"Yes," Job replied, "in spite of his early resentment of our coming, he seems to have adjusted. He carries us aloft to survey the land."

"You have no concerns about him?"

"Some … some. But I will let his actions speak for him. What is your thought?"

Apparently ignoring the question, 'Athaq continued.

"Have you seen others?"

Now Job was concerned. "Here? Leviathan's kin, here?"

"Yes."

"No … have you?"

"I have reason to believe they may come."

"How would they do that? Are they not physical, confined to the planet where Father has placed them?"

"That is a question that arises in our minds as well."

"And why?"

'Athaq paused, and Job could not read his face. "Yes, many questions arise. I will leave you now," is all he said, and Alnitak burst over the horizon, replacing the brightness of the Watcher with its own.

Job gathered the team later that day.

"Let's spread out, see what's here. I'll go north, along the near mountain range. Your preferences?"

"I'll do the coastline, and follow it north," I said. "Fishing," I explained, as the others looked at me.

"Send me east, to the far mountain range," said Julia. "Love to climb," she added in my direction.

John took the coastline to the south, and Linus wanted to explore the mountains to the south and east.

"Let's gather back here in 60 days," suggested Job. "Map it out, see what sorts of creatures are there, and learn what we can of what Father has in mind!" The next morning, we packed up and each set out to discover what we could of a brand new world.

That night, Gadol lifted off the ground as the second moon was disappearing below the horizon, and steadily climbed as high as he could maintain flight. From the highest point he could reach, he called out.

"Tontal!"

Now to wait, give Tontal time to climb out of his own atmosphere, away from the interference of the planet's mass. In a few minutes, the answer came.

"Who calls?"

"Gadol. Is Ruunt there?"

"Yes. How did you know?"

"'Athaq. They know he's missing."

"Do they know how he left?"

"No. How?"

"Slipstream," replied Tontal. "Almost killed him."

I'll bet it did, thought Gadol. However he managed it!

"Tell 'Athaq. Ask him to help."

"Help what?" exclaimed Gadol.

"Bring us all to 'Nsol. Alive!"

Gadol's endurance gave out, and he fell towards the planet, spreading his wings to coast as soon as the air was thick enough to support him.

Which did he prefer less? Being alone on this forsaken planet, with Adam's sons now invading, or being in the company of his brothers? Especially Tontal. Grief on legs. Pain, looking for an excuse to happen.

When he awoke the next morning and stumbled out to the pool, 'Athaq was waiting. He splashed into the pool and floated for a few minutes without acknowledging the Watcher, then slowly climbed out and settled on the grass.

"I know where Ruunt is."

'Athaq nodded. "With Tontal?"

Gadol stared at him. How could he have known? "Yes. Why?"

"It seemed likely," said 'Athaq, "except for being able to get there. Tontal enjoys having someone to obey him."

Gadol smiled. It was true.

"What is his purpose? Tontal, I mean."

This was far beyond what Gadol was willing to discuss.

"Tontal said I should ask your help…"

"Really."

"Can you bring them here?"

They looked at each other for long minutes.

"For what reason?" asked 'Athaq.

"Is it possible?"

"For what reason?" repeated the Watcher.

"Is it possible?"

"It is not allowed."

"I know that, Watcher! I did not ask if it were 'allowed'!"

'Athaq looked at the impatient beast before him, expressionless. "We will talk."

And Gadol was alone.

Ten

Julia set out across the valley, walking slowly to enjoy the day and not miss anything. A butterfly came alongside, fluttering around her head, and then wandered off on the breeze. Small blue flowers decorated the blue-green growth at her feet. She picked one, and smelled it. Shaped like a pansy, it offered a fragrance more like the magnolia blossom. She tucked it in her hat-band.

Soon she came alongside the stream that wandered across the valley to the sea. Here the banks were shallow, and the slope offered an easy climb down to the water. Dipping a hand in, she splashed the chill, clear water on her face, then cupped her hands to capture more, and drank. After filling a canteen she was ready to go on.

The sun stood above the peaks in the east, ahead of her and a little south. She pulled the hat brim down lower, and tilted her head down to shade her eyes. Looking for new life in the brush and foliage at her feet was more fun than looking into the sun.

A snake slipped past as she climbed up the bank. Yellow and orange, a type she had never seen.

"What are you?" she called. It quickly reappeared and curled up for closer inspection. Three or four feet long with a slender body, it did not have the triangular head that had always meant danger on earth. Its smooth skin sparkled in the morning sun with moisture from the dew.

"Beautiful, that's what you are!" she exclaimed. It uncoiled and slipped away, disappearing instantly in the deep grass.

Three hours later, she approached the foothills of the first range. Pulling out her map, she unrolled it.

"I'm ... here," she noted. The major peaks were marked, so the question was which path to take through them. From here, a gap seemed to open up a little south of her between two of the lower peaks. She rolled up the map and headed south along the range, moving slowly up the gentle slope as she walked. The lower trees seemed to be pine, with some fir and something like maple sprinkled in. Further up the slope birch stands showed white among the green. A breeze came off the mountain, whispering among the branches as it came down, bringing a mixture of smells that brought back memories of the Irish coastlands.

When a ravine crossed her path, she looked up. The trees were thick between her and the ridge, but the ravine seemed to run all the way up the cliff and the gap was there. She stepped into the ravine and started up into the trees. Undergrowth was well along, now, and it had not been long enough for animals to wear down trails in the fresh creation, so making her way up the steeper slopes of the foothills would take some time.

Pushing branches aside, she worked her way through the pine and fir, up into the birch, and found some oak at the higher slopes. Then she reached the gap through the ridge. A small space opened up at the crest. With the sun high overhead she spread a light blanket on the grass and settled down for a meal. Apples, an orange, some grapes. Half a loaf of ... rye? Must be. And water from the stream out in the valley.

She stretched out, and glanced at the sun.

"I wonder ..."

Instead of shielding her eyes, she let them grow accustomed to the unbearable brightness, until it seemed bearable, by squinting, then squinting less. Soon she was looking directly at the sun, perhaps twenty times the mass of the Earth's sun and much brighter. She focused more carefully. Along the edges, flares leaped up, and she could pick them out. The longer she looked, and the more carefully she focused, the more clearly she could see them. Letting her eyes wander into the bulk of the sun, she began to see swirling patterns, the tides of liquid fire that swept across the face of the star.

She looked more intently, amazed at what she could see now, things the eyes of her earthly body could not have endured. As she focused in, she realized she was seeing the inner layers of the star, deeper under the surface. Red swirls mixed with the orange and white, and above them the tongues of flame leaped from the surface many miles into space.

Deeper she looked. What was within the star, deeper still?

The core began to come into focus, a dense, dark red ball in the center of the visible star. At that level, thousands or millions of degrees of heat cooked all matter, and nuclear explosions were ongoing. The violence going on at the star's center amazed her. Moving her gaze out to the side, she could see the swirls of nuclear fire moving from the core out to the surface, and realized she was seeing not just visible flame, but the gases and radiation spewing out from the star to the rest of the universe. Wave upon wave of pure energy, and floods of whatever elements made up this sun, rocketed forth from it continually.

Relaxing her eyes, she closed them, and pulled the hat down over her face. She slept.

'Athaq paused halfway between 'Nsol and Alnitak. Thick clusters of stars surrounded him in every direction. The lightpaths ran among them, offering connections for all who could use them. The Universe was not the empty place man imagined it to be; physical bodies lacked the ability to see and hear reality. Angels, seraphim, the whole spiritual creation moved continuously along the paths, and music was everywhere. Dance and song were the natural expression of the spirit set free by the One, and the Universe continually celebrated His love.

'Athaq turned toward Mintaka, and then out to its planet 'Nsela. He came quietly to the surface of Tontal's planet and stood before the crevice leading to Tontal's cave. Dimming his radiance, he waited.

Tontal emerged.

"You are not 'Athelkan.'"

"True," replied 'Athaq. "We have not met since you awakened. I am 'Athaq, as you may remember, from Mintaka. Gadol is on the planet 'Nsol, in my region."

"Gadol has spoken with you."

"Yes."

"Will you do it?"

"Is Ruunt here?"

"Yes."

"May I see him?" asked the Watcher.

Tontal turned and walked slowly back into the crevice. In a few moments he emerged with Ruunt following. The smaller creature was covered in blisters, hide peeling in great scabs. His eyes were swollen, and he walked gingerly on the stones and gravel in the crevice opening. When he saw 'Athaq, he stopped.

"Who … is … this?" he croaked faintly.

Tontal did not respond, but watched 'Athaq examine the wounded creature.

"I do not wish to arrive in that condition, or worse," Tontal murmured.

"No, certainly not," agreed 'Athaq. "How did you get him here?"

"He found a way to get into the stream. I knocked him down as he came by."

"So you could easily have missed him, and he would have …"

"He would be dead."

They both looked at Ruunt, who had collapsed and fallen asleep.

"Can you protect us, and move us along the paths?"

"To join Gadol?"

"Yes."

"Are there others?"

"I have found Guntel, on 'Nra."

"And you wish him to come, as well."

"Yes."

"I will consider it."

Tontal bowed his head, and was suddenly alone with Ruunt at his feet.

A noise awoke her, and in the late afternoon light Julia saw Gadol perched nearby, watching her.

"You know, they don't think you are really one of them."

"What?"

"The men. I've heard them. You're a woman. Less, in every way."

She stared. "What in the world are you talking about?"

"They don't trust you to do your part. Not as strong. Not as smart. More mistakes. Need watching."

She looked at him, not knowing what to say.

"Forgive me. You were sleeping." In a single motion, he uncurled, pushed up, and climbed into the air.

"But ..." she said, and he was gone.

Looking about, she remembered where she was, and why. She stood, and stretched her arms high above her head. Mmm, felt good.

"Not as good ... what silliness." She rolled up the blanket, tucked it away, and pulled her hat onto her head. She pulled out one of the silken cords, and tied a bundle of red hair behind her neck to keep it off her shoulders.

"All right," she said to no one in particular.

Walking into the forest on the far side of the gap, she began descending. This side must get more rain, she thought. The trees are different. The ground cover is different ... more moss, and high weeds instead of the low grass.

Picking her way through a stand of elm, she came out upon a ledge overlooking the inner valley. There in the trees was the lake, as beautiful as a pearl found unexpectedly in a freshly opened oyster. The unruffled surface reflected the far mountains perfectly.

Plunging into the trees again, she hurried down the slope. Deer scattered, as she burst from a clump of underbrush. Stopping several yards away, they watched her intently.

"Welcome," she said. "Anything I can do for you?"

The buck swung his head from her to the herd, then back. He walked slowly towards her, and the others hesitated, then followed. She reached out to his face, as he approached. He stopped, motionless.

"Are you afraid of me?"

He walked closer, and she put a hand on his nose. He came up close, nuzzled her, then stepped back. Two fawns came to her, and rubbed against her legs.

"Aren't you precious!"

They scampered away, and the doe came shyly to her.

Julia sat down, to reduce any sense of threat they might feel. The doe bent her front legs, rested her weight for a moment on those knees, then lowered her body and lay down. Julia reached out to the doe and stroked her nose. This was apparently welcome, so she rubbed its ears and scratched the doe on the back where she could reach it. The doe rolled onto the ground, moving her back up next to Julia.

"Well, you know what you like, don't you!" She scratched the doe vigorously, until her arms gave out, then lay down against the mother deer, resting her head on its back. The doe did not move.

"Thank you. A fine pillow, indeed!"

After a few minutes she roused herself, and clambered to her feet. The doe did likewise.

As she brushed herself off, the buck gathered his family together and took them a few yards away. They turned and faced Julia.

"If you need help ..." the thought formed in Julia's mind, and she realized it was not her own thought being offered to the deer: it had arrived unbidden in her mind. The deer? Father, suggesting these are allies? She could not tell, but the message was clear. The buck would come, if she had need.

They drifted away, apparently foraging. She turned downhill and pressed on. Soon she emerged onto the beach around the lake, or rather, the wide lawn of flat grasses and flowers that served as a carpet all around it. There were yellow and blue flowers, and white blossoms in the distance, and a sweep of red and blue on the other side that could have been Indian paintbrush and bluebonnets in another world. What a landscape.

She walked to the water's edge, and peered in. Absolutely clear, absolutely still. In the shallows she saw minnows, and further out the dark shapes of larger fish.

Across the lake, in the deepening twilight, a bull elk stepped out onto the grass near the lake. Carefully surveying everything in sight, he walked majestically down to the water and stepped in. He waded out, stood knee deep, and drank long draughts of the rippling, clear water.

Others drifted out of the woods behind him and followed his lead down to the lake. Fifteen or more stood there as the last light of day faded from the sky and the stars blossomed.

"Is it my eyes, or clear air, or ... " Julia marveled at the sheer volume of stars visible. Faint ones, bright ones, spectacular ones. She looked more closely, and could pick out nebulae that only a telescope could have seen from Earth. Focusing more intently, she could see more and more detail.

"It's as though my eyes ... are a telescope ..." A flicker of shadow across her vision brought her back to the present, and she realized Gadol had flown overhead. A few moments later she felt him drop to the ground several yards away, and heard the wings fold and the claws tear the ground.

"Hello, Gadol."

"Yes."

A long silence ensued. She turned to him.

"What do you want this time, Gadol?"

"If you are hurt, they won't come for you. Not worth it. You know that."

"Gadol, that's ridiculous. I don't want to hear any more of it."

He stared at her, and she decided to change the subject.

"Did you know we've named some constellations? I think that one is the Throne," she said, finally locating it and pointing.

No comment from her visitor.

"Look over there," she said, pointing down the valley to a formation due south. "We call that Leviathan."

"What?" His shout was almost a roar. He looked where she pointed, to a cluster of stars in a rough S shape.

"Yes," he said, after looking for a moment. "Yes."

"He is your ... father?"

Gadol was silent for a moment. "Yes."

"Will you see him again?"

"Of course," replied Gadol, but there was no certainty at all in his answer. "Of course," he repeated.

"Why do you think so?"

"Because He can't ..." Gadol stopped, and his voice calmed. "Because."

Julia decided she had touched a raw nerve that should be left alone.

Or maybe not.

"Will he repent?"

Silence followed, but she felt a new heat in the air. Gadol stood and paced, moving twenty yards away into the darkness.

"Will you?" she continued, looking in his direction in the starlight.

A sound that may have been "humph" was the last she heard.

Guntel was sleeping, mostly submerged in the surf, when 'Athaq stood before him. He woke with a start as the brilliant light flooded the night, and stared at the Watcher.

"Which one are you?"

"'Athaq."

"And you are here because …?"

"Tontal wants you."

Guntel rolled over in the surf, and lay facing away from the Watcher.

"I can take you."

He rolled back over, and slowly stood up. "Do I want to go?"

'Athaq smiled. "Do you want to stay here?"

Guntel looked around at the darkness, seeing in his mind the planet he had grown to hate.

"Even less."

"As I thought. Are you ready?"

"What do you intend to do?"

"You know the paths between the suns."

"I knew them. I am in flesh, Watcher, I cannot use them anymore."

"But I can."

"And carry me?"

"Yes."

"Do it."

"You will sleep."

When Guntel awoke he was again half-submerged, but in a pool he did not recognize, and his hide was hot to the touch. A headache raged in the front of his head, and every muscle was sore beyond belief.

"Did I fall off a cliff? Why do I hurt so badly ..." Then memory returned.

He climbed out of the pool, and stood looking around.

Gadol emerged from the cave in front of him.

"Gadol, is that you?"

"It is, brother. Welcome. I wondered how long it would take for you to wake."

"How long have I been here?"

"Three days. The Watcher brought you. Do you hurt?"

"In every part."

Gadol laughed. "And you slept?"

Eleven

The next morning, Julia woke alongside the lake and discovered a mountain lion sleeping just uphill from her. Stilling her instinctive fears, she sat up slowly and watched the big cat. It woke at the noise of her movement. After looking at her for a long moment, it stretched, rolled to its feet, and sat up. They looked at each other. Finally the animal stood, yawned, and walked slowly up to her, until it stood with its mouth inches away from her face. The big mouth opened, and it licked her with an enormous tongue, from the neck all the way up to the top of her head, one time. Then it turned, and walked slowly into the woods, as though she did not exist.

"Unbelievable. Just amazing."

She stripped down and walked to the lake, testing the water. Cold, but not freezing. Not as bad as the Irish Sea! She dove in and swam long, lazy strokes out into the lake. When the water was deep enough that she could not stand, she dove to the bottom, and found all manner of stones shining in the morning light as it filtered down through the water. Striped ones, green and gold and blue ones. Color shone everywhere. She picked one up that seemed to have a star pattern on it, and came up for air. Using a sidestroke so she could carry the stone, she swam back to the shore, and walked up to her pack. The blanket served as a towel, and she used it to work the water out of her hair and dry off. She dressed, and tucked the stone away. Combing her hair out so it would dry more completely, she hung her hat around her neck and thought about where to go next.

To Father, she thought. That's where I should go next!

Closing her eyes and lifting her hands, she entered before the Throne, her favorite place. The warmth of his welcome drew her in, and for the next hour, she knew nothing of the planet 'Nsol. Standing before Father, worshiping, accepting his love, that was enough. That was always enough.

As the second sun added its heat to the day she set out down the valley, intending to spend some time on the level ground before heading up to the next range. Orchards seem to have sprung up almost randomly, with one variety of fruit blending into another as the trees changed. The oranges were large and soft, with more pulp than she was used to and incredibly good. She pulled one down, peeled it, and slowly ate each segment. On a whim, she rubbed the inside of the peel against her face and arms, and felt a stimulating refreshment. A flock of birds came by, white, but as big as hawks. She tossed a fragment of the peel up to them, and one wheeled down to catch it. He called to his mates, and they all swirled down around her, circling, waiting. She tore the peel into small pieces and tossed them up, one at a time. Suddenly she realized her efforts to spread the food around, to make sure a different bird got each one, were unneeded. As each soaring dove (as she named them without thinking) took a piece, it rose to a higher circle and others came in for their bit.

"If that's not evidence of the healing, I'm a Scottish bar-maid!" she laughed.

When the peel was gone, she held up empty hands. They swooped past her in apparent farewell, and headed north again.

A stream appeared to her left as she walked. She wondered if it had come from the lake behind her. Walking over to it, she noticed golden minnows darting about, and now and then something she'd never seen - a larger fish with a splash of red down its sides.

"He'll probably have a name for that, and even some bait in his pocket," she grinned.

Feeling great, and fresh from the meal, she began to trot. The light pack on her back seemed to weigh nothing at all, and she began to run, a loping, steady run that was not a sprint, but was fast enough to leave her winded in minutes ... in the old days.

And she ran. The sun climbed higher, and the smaller sun rose to the south of it. On she ran, and the suns climbed above her and began settling into the western sky. On she ran, not tired at all, over miles upon miles of grassy valley, wooded slopes, and past towering mountains on either side.

As the setting suns disappeared behind the western peaks, she stopped, amazed. The open sky would be light for some time to come, but the shadows were cool now, and the stream on her left had become a wide river, moving quickly.

"I want to go there", she said, looking up at the eastern range. "How shall I cross you?" The river spoke no word in reply, yet she felt a friendliness about it, perhaps just the companionship of having run side by side for these many miles.

"You won't help me, will you?" she pouted at it, as though it could answer, and she almost imagined it could.

An eagle drifted down in a wide, slow circle over the grassland across the river, and moved out into even wider circles as it came lower. When it was almost to the ground, it turned, glided across the river and dropped to the lush grass some 20 feet away.

"Hello!" she exclaimed. "How handsome you are!"

The great bird ducked its head under a wing for a moment, then looked at her, cocking its head to one side, blinking, studying her.

"Say ... would you carry my pack and clothes across the stream for me?"

The eagle turned toward the stream, then back to her, then ducked its head a couple more times, then slowly walked a wandering path up to within a few feet of her. She stepped towards it, reaching out a hand, and it stood watching.

"Am I about to get bit?" she wondered. As her hand came close, its head suddenly jerked forward at her, and she pulled back. But the eagle simply held its head still. For her to touch? She reached out again, and stroked the white feathers on top of its head and down its back.

"Well, thank you," she said. "Is that a 'yes'?"

The eagle stepped back and stood there, as though waiting.

"Well. I guess it's my turn!"

Quickly stripping off her clothes, she pulled out a cord and tied them into a bundle with her pack and hat. With some extra length she made a loop, a sort of handle, in case the eagle would use that. Finally ready, she and the eagle stood looking at each other for a moment.

"Here I go. Follow me?" She turned, walked to the river bank, and eased a foot in.

"Oooh, it's a little cooler now! Whoo!" Wading in to her knees, then on to waist deep, she decided it was time to commit. She dove under the water, swimming across the current and being carried downstream by it. Stretching out in a lazy sidestroke, she looked up at the deep blue, almost purple sky, where hundreds of stars were already brighter than the early evening sky.

The water didn't seem so chilly after a few minutes, and she stretched out into a full crawl stroke, relishing the exercise and refreshment. Minnows swept around her, playing with her toes. Helpless to stop them, she decided to enjoy the nibbles best she could.

Finally she reached the eastern shore, and put her feet down on the smooth gravel of the river bed. Walking carefully up the side, she had to pull herself up the bank by the ferns and ivy that grew there, as the bank was steep and slippery. She pulled herself over the edge, rolled onto her back, and lay there to dry.

She heard a movement in the grass close to her head. Startled, she began to quickly get up, but caught herself.

"When will I finally believe?" she chided herself.

Slowly turning over, she came face to face with the largest box turtle she had ever seen. Its nose inches away from hers, it was at least half her size and twice her weight. Catching her breath, she managed to stay in place.

"Umm ... hello?"

It looked at her for another half minute or so, then settled down, pulled itself into its shell, and continued to watch her from inches away.

"Maybe I should do the same," she grinned. Moving slowly so as not to startle it, she pushed up to her feet and looked for the eagle. He stood close by, with the clothes and pack in front of him.

"My thanks," she said. "Do I know your name?" Looking at him for a moment, it seemed to form in her mind. Swalea? Yes, that felt right.

"Swalea? Have I heard Him right?" The eagle nodded its head once and swept up into the air, circling wider and wider until it was lost to sight.

"Swalea. Thank you. I'll see you again, I hope," she whispered, as she combed out her hair and gathered up her things.

"And you?"

Turning to the great brown and green shell and the reluctant soul inside, she asked, "What shall I call you? And how did you get so big, so fast?"

It seemed somehow to radiate its pleasure at the compliment, and the name 'Mmoff' seemed to be right.

"Interesting," she said, "I've never known anyone by that name either. Take care, Mmoff, and be blessed."

Walking up the wooded slope that came very near the river here, she found a secluded place on the forest floor and settled in, ready for a good night's sleep. Smoothing out a place between the oak roots, she spread her pallet and stretched out. Stars blazed above the branches, and the soft symphony of the deeper woods washed gently over her.

I began exploring the canyons and ridges running along the coast for miles north of our cave as the others scattered across the face of the planet to explore and map other areas. I felt a deep sense of peace as we parted; I had no concern about snakebite, wild animals, a broken leg, getting lost, or any of the many things that would have concerned me in earlier life. It was not a sense that we could not be hurt, I suppose, just that the joy of the Father ran in our veins, and the stain of sin was not on the planet.

We did not need to carry paper or maps or pens, though Julia seemed to enjoy doing so. We looked, and remembered, and there seemed no limit to the detail that we could carry in our minds. Maps could be drawn whenever we wished, once we had been through the land, and with complete accuracy, our memories undimmed by the passage of time.

I climbed with a strength and grip that amazed me. I needed barely a finger-hold to move up a sheer wall, and I could see with such clarity the texture of the rock faces that I could map out a route all the way up, standing on the floor of a canyon. This was the way climbing was meant to be!

I walked the high ridges, moving north from our base. I loved looking down on the sea, hearing the distant roar of the surf when waves were high, and smelling the salty breeze. Gulls circled around me as though in greeting, as they moved up and down the coastline.

About 50 miles north, I could see islands in the distance. Suddenly I was intrigued. Could I reach them? I began working my way down a ravine that seemed to lead to the shoreline. The grass of the high mesa gave way to tumbled rock and gravel, and the weeds that grew with very little soil. Some large boulders blocked the way, and I discovered I could jump down as far as fifteen, maybe twenty feet, and land comfortably on my feet and stay balanced. Did we weigh less here? Or was it just the resilience of the "new body," undiminished by the wear and tear of earthly life?

Sliding down a grassy slope halfway down to the surf, I landed face to face with something like a cougar. Its large, muscular body was poised and alert a few feet away, watching me slip down the slope unaware of its presence. The smooth, tawny skin of the big cat shone in the hot sun, and I think it must have blended in with the color of the rock and sand around him. I had the definite sense that he enjoyed my surprise, though I can't actually say I saw him smile. But I might have.

I sat there and looked at him. Easily twice my weight, he blinked a couple of times, then sat where he was, returning my gaze.

"Have we met?"

He tilted his head, then licked a paw. Apparently not.

"Do you have a name?"

He looked intently at me, and I had the sense he was trying to suggest one, or tell me what it was. "It's all right, I wouldn't give you one that you didn't like!" He seemed to relax with that assurance, and went back to licking the paw.

"How about 'Sulan'?" I suggested.

He seemed pleased. He stood, bowed his head slowly and raised up, looking intently at me. Suddenly he leaped towards me; I had no time to react. He soared past my shoulder onto a rock ledge and sprang up the cliff-side, leaping from boulder to boulder, making his way to the top. I watched his powerful, graceful, and almost silent ascent until he was out of sight.

Gadol appeared unexpectedly in the ravine before me, as it opened up around a bend.

"What are you doing?" he asked, in that gravelly voice. Suddenly I was very uncomfortable with the situation.

"We're learning what the planet looks like, and deciding how to manage it."

"Want to see it from higher up?"

It was a common event now for us to ride his back, as we surveyed various parts of the planet, so I had no obvious reason to refuse. And this territory was new to me, so learning it from ground level was certainly the hard way. A storm was rolling in, and the wind had kicked up; I did not want to spend very much time up there, but it would be helpful. And I loved to fly.

I unfolded a pallet from my pack, and retrieved some cord. In a few minutes we were lifting up over the valley.

"John was never born, was he?" asked Gadol. I was stunned. He had never shown any interest at all in our backgrounds.

"No, actually … why?"

"So he never knew Earth, or what it was like to live there."

"No."

"Julia … does it give her any trouble? The only woman, among you men?"

This was getting decidedly uncomfortable.

"I don't think so. Listen, put me down over there, by that stream. I want to explore it at ground level."

No response.

"Gadol?"

"Hold on," he replied with a hardness to his voice I had not heard before, and plunged down towards the ocean.

"Where are you going?" I yelled.

There was no answer. We fell, arrow straight, like a rocket fired from a barrel, and flew with no resistance, faster, faster, towards the heavy, pounding surf pushed by the approaching storm.

He'll flatten out at the surface, like he normally does, I thought. But we accelerated as the sea approached, and instinctively I grabbed a breath and clutched his back even closer. We slammed into the water, and it was all I could do to concentrate on holding on.

After a few seconds of plunging deeper, we seemed to turn and go level. But his wings were folded close to his body, squeezing my legs roughly as though he were making sure I would not get loose. I could not open my eyes, with the salty water and the pressure of the depth. I supposed we were at least twenty, maybe fifty feet down, but I really had no idea. It got darker, then completely dark. Just when I could hold my breath no longer, we burst from the surface into sweet, sweet air.

I heard the water sloshing around us as we climbed up from the sea, and his breathing, and my own gasping for air, but I could see nothing, and I heard nothing else.

He still crushed my legs against his rough sides, with no regard for my comfort, or, it seemed to me, whether I would even be able to walk again. There was no point in asking him again what he was doing, so I simply endured, and waited.

He walked for some distance. I could hear his claws scraping against rock, and occasionally it seemed he walked on sand. My eyes did not adjust. There was no light to adjust to, just the total darkness and a feeling of being underground.

Finally he turned and seemed to stoop. With a twist and a shake, he threw me off. I fell hard upon cold, rough stone that sloped down and away, and I rolled over against an unexpected wall. There was noise of scraping, maybe the dragging of something heavy, and then receding steps as he quickly left.

Twelve

Julia worked her way up the hillside and topped a ridge that opened up a view higher into the foothills of the deeper mountain range. The lake behind her, she took a deep breath and raised her hands in praise to the Creator who had imagined and then spun forth such beauty. Standing with her eyes closed, she felt the cool wind coming down from the snowy peaks, and the late afternoon sun warming her back.

She looked again at the panorama before her. "I've never seen anything more beautiful," she murmured.

A swoosh behind her startled her, and as she turned to see what manner of eagle or hawk had approached, great claws closed around her waist and jerked her off her feet. Suddenly she was well up in the air and climbing fast. She looked up to see the belly and throat of Gadol as he swept his great wings above her and rose rapidly above the trees.

"What are you doing?" she shouted, but got no answer. The wings pumped, the air got colder, and the distant mountain peaks were not so distant. Most of an hour passed. Far above the tree line now and still climbing, he swung a wide circle and rose higher, still higher, now on the backside of the nearest peaks, out of sight of the lower ranges, the lake, and the broad valley where they first stood.

She hugged her arms around her, shivering in the high altitude and approaching night.

They approached a steep cliff face and she saw an opening ahead, a small black space above thousands of feet of sheer drop, far from any vegetation. Gadol spread his wings as they approached it, and tossed her into the darkness, freeing up his feet for landing.

She fell roughly and rolled across the floor of a small cave, bouncing on gravel and other debris, tumbling into a pile.

When she pushed up from the floor, got to her knees, and looked back, Gadol was perched at the edge of the cliff. A moment later, he was gone.

What in the world? she thought. What is he doing?

Facing away from the setting sun, she looked out on a majestic view, ranges of mountains to the east that seemed never to end. Further south, though, the peaks grew lower, and settled out into broad, low hills with valleys and perhaps the glint of a river among the fog banks she could see.

Turning, she inspected her new home. Bones littered the floor, animal bones.

"He's been eating, it appears."

She tossed all the bones she could find out the cave opening, trying not to listen to the sounds of their bouncing against the cliff far below. There was no way to climb out, from what she had seen. Moving deeper into the cave, she found a smaller alcove to the back that might preserve warmth a little better than the larger open area, and nothing more.

Silence.

I slowly unfolded from the pile I had landed in and felt for damage. Shoulder bruised, arms and hands scraped up, one knee hurting and beginning to swell. No ribs broken, that I could tell. Felt like blood on my face, or something slimy from the water. I tasted it. Blood.

The unrelenting darkness pressed in, and the silence hammered on my ears. I spoke, and there was no echo, no sense of an open space.

I stood, carefully, testing whether my legs could hold any weight. If I favored the right knee, I could stand all right. I took a step. Another step, suddenly shifting weight to the other leg, and I realized I wouldn't be walking far, any time soon. By choice, anyway.

Feeling for the wall I had crashed into, I quickly found it, and felt along it. Curving to the right, it led me to a corner where there seemed to be an opening that had been blocked. From there, the surface was no longer rock, but some sort of heavy brush or plant material.

Stabbing my hand unexpectedly on a thorn, I pulled back. Were there any sticks here? I felt around the ground, and found nothing. I took my shirt off, wadded it up, and used it as a glove to feel the direction of this brush wall. It was not much wider than Gadol's body, and quickly I was back to a stone surface, still curving to the right. Within not many steps, I came to brush again, and realized I had completed the circle. I was in a closet. A closet of stone and thorns, perhaps a few hundred feet below the surface.

I reached up, and immediately touched rock, damp rock, just above my head.

I sat. Hurting, I measured the length of the open floor, and discovered there was just room for me to lie down.

I slept for some unknown time, and awoke shivering with a sudden sense of panic, not knowing where I was. Memory flooded back, and I lay still, listening.

The darkness was complete. No sound, no light, nothing.

A single drop fell on me from the damp, chilly stone above, startling me in the silence and total blackness.

I tensed to turn over, to lift myself off the cold, smooth rock, but a stab of pain overwhelmed me.

"God," I thought, "what's going on? Where am I?" Everything in me suddenly reached out for Him, for Home.

For an answer.

In the deep silence following my desperate, silent cry, a slow rhythm began seeping into my bones. It was not yet audible, but I felt it, a slow, insistent drumbeat, gradually increasing in tempo. Another rhythm joined it, faster, more complex, and higher. Now I could hear them, and a single high note began, a long, pure, crystalline call to worship.

A compelling, pulsing melody began, and everything in me seemed to rise, to respond in a surge of delight that cared not about my pain and despair. A joy beyond all circumstances suddenly poured into my heart, and in the freezing darkness I began to laugh.

A space opened in my mind as though a curtain had drawn back to reveal an empty stage. In that space an image emerged, a vision that was not a vision, a window through immeasurable distance. Thousands stood in rapt silence, facing into blinding light, with expressions of awe and joy on their faces.

Then a few stepped out from the ranks of white-robed angels and began to dance.

As their grace and beauty brought tears to my eyes and an improvised song of worship to my lips, I realized once again the peace of knowing Him, and being His. The joy of being loved by the Creator himself. The freedom to take the adventure he sends, and trust him for the outcome.

He had answered me. He had shown me "what was going on," not where I was, but where it really mattered. And it was enough. I listened to their song, and watched their dance, and slept again.

The next time I awoke, the bruises were gone, and there was no trace of dried blood on my face or head. I stood carefully, and found I could put weight on the knee.

"Thank you, Father," I whispered.

Linus moved quickly across the plains. When he crossed the now-familiar stream, he laughed to see the abundance of fish, frogs, lizards, and flowers now populating the stream and the banks that were so empty on their arrival. Turning south along the foothills of the first mountain range, he could see much higher mountains ahead, and began angling up the slope into the first line of trees. When the two suns disappeared under the western horizon and the night sky blazed with uncountable stars, he bedded down under the pines with a happy heart and fell asleep quickly.

A cacophony of birds and crickets woke him early. After a breakfast of apples and grapes, he struck out for higher ground, still moving south. Much as he enjoyed the invigorating brilliance of these two suns, the shade of the woods was welcome. Birds called from the branches, and an occasional butterfly glowed brightly when caught by the sunbeams filtering through the leaves.

A cliff rose suddenly before him, and seemed to have cracks in its face. Searching for possible openings, Linus found one, and stepped into a quiet, open space completely hidden from the forest outside. A light from above revealed another opening, a larger one, somewhere on the top of the cliff, and the reflecting light spread into tunnels opening in all directions from where he stood.

He looked around. A streak of red clay marked the wall behind him, where the crack opened into the forest. If he walked straight away from that, it should be easy to find on the way back. Facing forward, he chose a large tunnel that seemed to offer level ground and an easy path to explore. In two or three minutes of steady walking, it opened into another, larger cavern, then narrowed down and continued. He walked on. The air seemed fresh.

A scrape of gravel behind him caused him to stop, turn, and listen. Nothing appeared. He walked on. Going through a small opening, he came to a downward sloping floor in a room with the feel of a very high ceiling. He began down the slope, and lost his footing on loose gravel. Sliding down, he found a few places to catch a grip and slow the fall, but it was not terribly steep. He slid to the bottom.

Very little light penetrated this far, and he peered into the largest room yet of the caverns he had discovered. A few feet from where the slope had leveled out he found a stream that bubbled and swirled quickly through the cavern from an unseen source to unseen destinations. The light from the opening above that first cave had diffused through the first few rooms closest to the opening, but now he was far enough from the entrance that he was having trouble seeing, even as his eyes adjusted amazingly well to almost total darkness.

The room appeared to go on quite a bit further, and he began walking along the stream, walking further into the darkness, counting his steps and calling out to listen for echoes. He almost stumbled several times, and the uneven floor surprised him. Finally he sat down to rest a bit and to decide how to proceed.

The time in Rome was difficult, being pursued at times by soldiers. They had been driven into some very interesting places. He had grown to love the underground caverns of Rome, and these reminded him of old memories and good friends.

A crashing sound behind him startled him to his feet, and all the remaining light vanished.

"What ..." he exclaimed, then froze, listening. There was no further sound.

Without moving, he thought about what was around him, which way he was facing, and which way the opening was. He tried to imagine the scene that was just before him, and where the stream lay.

He turned and walked carefully, remembering the tricky surface of the cave bottom he had just crossed. But the opening was many feet away and up a slope of loose rock; how would he find it?

The opening must have been closed. How?

There had been nothing near the opening that could have fallen over it, and nothing that would have caused a collapse. It must have been covered on purpose. By whom?

"Is anyone there?" he shouted.

No answer. The echo of his voice returned from multiple directions.

All right, he thought, let's go find that opening.

Listening to the stream on his left, he stepped carefully, one foot after the other, testing for solid ground under his boot before setting his weight down on each foot. He walked slowly, carefully counting, several times having to pause and find a better place for the next step. Twice he thought he heard scraping or shuffling sounds, but they were distant and muffled.

After several minutes and the right number of steps, he decided he must be near the opening. Turning to the right, he began feeling with his feet, stepping carefully, testing for the uprising bank of shale and gravel he had slid down to get into the cavern.

How would he get back up, in the dark? If it were still light, he could see the few handgrips that the slope offered, but he could see nothing in the dark.

Slowly, slowly he moved, one step at a time, hand reaching out for a grip.

Suddenly the ground gave way under his back foot, and when he stepped down with the other foot, there was nothing there. He fell, tumbling, and something struck his head and back. He drifted in and out of consciousness for hours, and his mind wandered back to an earlier time.

Thirteen

Linus edged and shoved and slid through the mob, pushing as little as he could, but constantly being pushed into others and having to mutter excuses. Being the biggest spectator in the crowd didn't help. A blistering sun made everyone irritable, and the guards made sure the ones in front didn't want to be.

Where was the prisoner? He finally saw Paul, and marveled at how small he was. The rabbi, and really everyone at that little synagogue, had talked of no one else for weeks. But there he was, and hardly tall enough to be seen between the guards.

Linus followed until the iron gates clanged shut and the bar dropped on the inside. Paul and the group clustered around him disappeared into the buildings, on the way to see Caesar if you could believe the crowds.

After a few minutes of sweating and pushing against one another to get a better view, the men around him apparently realized there was nothing to see, and began drifting away. It had been a great excuse to slip away from the stink of the tannery and the heat of the smelting fires and the noise of the markets, but it was past time for them to get back. Linus crouched against a stone wall in a bit of shade, and waited.

When the sun was touching the second story roof across the plaza, his patience was rewarded. A single Roman guard slipped out through a side entrance near the gate, and Paul was with him, close enough that Linus could not see whether the wrist chain was still holding him hostage. They came directly towards him.

When they were about to pass him, Linus stood up, began walking, and fell in beside Paul.

"May I walk with you?"

The guard started to push him away with a foul curse, but Paul held a hand up, and the guard stopped instantly. Linus had never seen the like.

"Certainly! I wish you could join me for dinner," replied Paul, and the guard stepped back. "I have no one to eat with, and would enjoy the company. But the cells are not where you would like spending your evenings!"

A few days later, Linus went back to the palace and inquired about jobs serving in the jail. The soldier at the archway into the lower palace courts stared.

"You want to do … what?" he asked.

"Work in the jails. Where the man from Tarsus is, the Jew."

He laughed. "You would do that, just to be close to him?"

"Yes."

"Well, don't waste your time! He's not here."

"What?"

"Not going to be in this rat hole. He's out. Got a place on Appian Way, I hear. Octavius stays there to guard him. Now go on!"

"Pretty easy job…." muttered the guard, as Linus walked quickly out of the hated building.

"Appian Way…" Linus looked about, trying to remember where that might be. Down and east, maybe, toward the synagogue? That would make sense.

The next day, trudging through the dust and August heat, he found the house. A plain structure, with the usual courtyard in the center, rooms around the side and a window box of wilted flowers doing its best to entice strangers onto the porch, the house drew no attention to itself. But half of Rome must have been inside!

He squeezed onto the porch and eased into the front room, but could go no further. Paul sat at the far end of the room on a pallet and his visitors filled every inch of the house. The first thing that struck Linus was the silence; how could that many men be so silent? Then he realized: Paul was speaking, but in a voice so strained and soft he could hardly be heard. This must have been going on for days!

The stooped, wiry man just in front of Linus screamed in frustration, at whatever he just heard.

"No! God is one! How can this Jesus be anything more than a man? Blasphemy!"

All around him, men stirred, angry murmurs running across the room. Paul sipped from a mug as he waited for silence. He looked calmly around the room, smiled at the people sitting in the window over the high stairway, and looked at the man who had shouted at him.

A voice came from the corner, where Linus could not see the speaker. "Josiah, it does say 'We' in the account of Adam, you do remember that, and making Adam in 'Our' image? Who was the 'We', and the 'Our'? Not the angels, surely, Adam was not made in the image of angels!"

The room exploded in frustrated and amused reaction, some laughing, some shouting answers. Paul sipped his drink and waited. The crowd grew more agitated, and some who had been sitting rose to their feet. Others shouted at them to sit down, demanding to be able to see Paul. Just when it appeared to Linus that the meeting was going to disintegrate, Paul rose.

"Shh! What is he doing?"

Everyone turned their attention to him, as he beckoned a young man to rise.

"Is that your father with you?"

"Yes, sir, yes it is…" the man responded, haltingly, looking around him.

"He does not see well?"

"No … sir … Paul … he cannot see you at all. Isn't that right, Father?" Turning back to Paul, he added, "His name is Tyrus."

The older man nodded, looking towards Paul but certainly not seeing him.

"Bring him here."

All conversation stopped abruptly, and the room plunged into total silence. The day was almost gone; men had lit whatever lamps were close by as Paul was teaching. The scent of olive oil drifted through the diffused orange light, and a warm breeze refreshed those close to the windows. A man down the street shouted at friends, and two or three answered him from further away.

But in this room nothing moved, save the older man and his son as they stepped carefully through the men seated between them and Paul. Linus realized he was holding his breath, and began breathing again, smiling at himself.

Paul reached out to the stooped elder, drew him close, and turned him so all could see. "Would you like to see, Tyrus?" The man looked towards him without responding for a long moment, then tears began seeping from his old eyes.

"Yes, Paul. Yes, I would. You can do that?"

Paul laughed, the easy laugh of someone completely comfortable in himself. "No, no, I certainly cannot. But I know someone who can!"

Laying his hands on the man, Paul looked up and waited. Not a person in the room stirred. Finally Paul looked at him intently, and said, "Now. See. Receive the gift of God, and look at your son!"

Tyrus closed his eyes, and Paul turned him towards his son. He stood there until Linus was about to shout at him, and finally opened his blind eyes again. His son looked intently at his father's eyes, and then stared, and began to jump up and down.

"Father, what's happening? I can see the color of your eyes, the color that has been gone for years!"

Tyrus nodded, and reached out to his son's face. The old finger traced his son's eyebrows, and his nose, and his cheek. Then he turned slowly around, looking out over the room. "Joseph?" he said, and someone answered, "Here."

"Machir?"

"Asher?"

As each name was spoken, someone answered, and Tyrus looked at friends he had apparently never seen, weeping openly, staring at them with joy and amazement written all over his face.

Finally he turned all the way back around, and looked at Paul.

"Paul."

"Here," answered the apostle, just as all Tyrus' friends had done. Tyrus stepped forward and grabbed him, squeezing him until Paul begged for release.

Then the entire room somehow surged forward to reach him, and Tyrus was buried in the hugs and greetings of people he might never have recognized until they spoke.

Linus slipped outside to laugh and jump and spin around, delighted and amazed at what he had seen. "God, you are in this, you really are!" he laughed, and jumped again, and again. Others caught his joy, and began dancing around and shouting with him. "Hosannah, hosannah!" they cried, running up and down the rough pavement of the narrow street.

"He's teaching again," came the word from the front door, and they all rushed to squeeze back in. Others came from nearby houses, drawn by the noise, and soon the windows were full as well.

"Now," said Paul, "where were we?"

When the sun rose next morning, Paul was listing the prophecies fulfilled at the crucifixion of Jesus, making his case for the Messiah stronger and stronger. But many were getting sleepy at that point, and men were stretching and yawning each time Paul paused to sip or take a bite of something.

Paul said, "Men, we have talked long. Let us retire to our homes and families. We will talk more of these things in days to come. But remember, the kingdom of God does not consist in talk, but in Power."

No one had a response to that. They had seen the reality of his words.

Linus sought Paul out the next day. The teacher sat on the porch, with five men sitting around him or leaning on the columns. Bits of pomegranate littered the dishes around them.

"Too late for lunch!" said Paul, as Linus stepped up.

Linus smiled, pulling off his cap. "My name is Linus," he offered, "and I'd like to be in your service for a time. May I stay with you, and take care of some of your needs as they arise?"

"Can you write?" asked Paul. Linus nodded. "Can people read what you write?" laughed Paul, and Linus nodded, sharing in the laugh.

"They tell me so, in any case!"

Paul looked around at the others. They smiled, and the tallest of them said, "Should we tell him?"

Linus looked from one to the other. "Please do!"

Paul leaned back on the step. "I had just told these gentlemen that I needed someone to stay here, and in particular to help with my letters.

My eyes are bad enough now, I need someone else to manage the quill for me!"

"But you healed the eyes of Tyrus, I saw it!"

Paul shrugged. "God did that, not me. Jesus said he just did whatever he saw his Father doing, and that's what I did. That's what I always do."

The unspoken question drifted on the still air.

"He hasn't offered to heal me," Paul replied simply. "And I can't do it myself!" He looked around at the group. "But if you see Him doing that, let me know!" Everyone laughed.

Turning to Linus, he said, "Yes, you may stay here, and I welcome you. Apparently that's one prayer He has decided to answer!"

That evening Linus joined them for supper. After soup was served and the eating slowed down a bit, the men began talking of this and that.

"Paul?" ventured Linus, in a silent moment.

Paul looked at him, waiting.

"You were a Pharisee."

"Yes. None better!"

"So, pretty strong on keeping the Jewish law, doing everything right?"

"None better! Of course, I say it to my shame, now."

The men around murmured. This was a familiar conversation, it appeared.

Linus frowned. "Why would you ever be ashamed of doing things right?"

Paul smiled. "Think of a time when you were proud of doing something right, doing it really well."

Linus rested his chin on clasped fingers. "All right."

"Now, think about why you did it, why you tried so hard to get it right, why it was important to you."

"Because it was the right thing to do. It was … good to do. It helped people."

"That's fine, Linus. I'm glad. Now think more deeply. Think about what was in your heart, besides wanting to help people."

Linus closed his eyes. Paul returned to his soup, and his friend on the other side passed a loaf of warm bread to him.

Linus smelled the bread, and opened his eyes. Paul was extending a platter to him with half a loaf, butter, and honey.

"Oh, that smells wonderful. Is this all mine?" The men laughed. "There's plenty, young man, and you look like you need to fill up! That's yours!"

"So?" asked Paul, when Linus had his mouth absolutely full. Linus looked at him wide-eyed as the men laughed. "I caught you, didn't I! Finish your bite, Linus, I'm in no hurry. Have you thought about it?"

"I guess I was proud of being able to do it," he said slowly, after washing down the honey and bread. "I wanted them to think well of me."

"Now you're seeing what was in your heart. Care to go deeper?"

"I don't know," smiled Linus. "I'm not liking what I'm seeing!"

"We never do," exclaimed a younger man across the table. "What's in the heart is what comes out of your mouth when you don't keep the reins tight!"

Linus turned back to Paul. "But you followed the law, and the customs, and honored the holidays, and did it all for God! Your heart was right, in all those things."

Paul shook his head. "I thought so. I did. And when I tried to put the Christians in jail, I was doing God's work!"

Linus stared at him. "I don't know about that. Did you really?"

He nodded. "Had them beaten. One of them was stoned by the mob, and I was glad."

Silence held the table for a full minute.

"But … but your heart. Was it not right, before God? You believed they were wrong!"

"I thought it was. But I was proud of how right I was, and proud of how well I kept the law, and proud of being from the best family and the best school, and being … perfect."

"Outwardly," commented the man on the other side. "Outwardly."

"Yes," murmured Paul. "Outwardly."

"What happened? How did you change?" asked Linus.

"I had never actually seen Jesus. Never really heard him speak. But when I was almost to Damascus, going to jail some of his followers there, He introduced himself to me."

"Was he alone? Was he on the road too?"

Paul laughed. "He IS the road!"

Linus frowned, and waited.

"No, this was after he had been crucified, after he had returned, after he had talked with hundreds of his followers!" Paul leaned back, and sighed. "So many times I could have met him… so many times. And I did not."

"But on the road? What did he look like?"

Everyone but Linus laughed. He looked around.

"Like a flash of lightning, so bright the sun was dimmed! Like a blow to the head that leaves you breathless and confused! Like … I don't know what he looks like. I saw a light so bright I was blind for days afterwards, and I heard his voice as clearly as I hear yours."

"What did he say?" whispered Linus.

"The voice asked why I was persecuting him. I said, 'Who are you?' and he replied, 'I am Jesus.'"

"I was there," said the younger man across the table. "I saw the light, but the voice was just thunder, I could hear no words in it. It knocked him down to the ground! We thought lightning had killed him! And then he struggled to rise to his knees, and began talking to the thunder… and it answered him!"

He stared at Paul.

"But he could not see us then, or the Lord."

"And he told you then … about your heart? About what you had been doing?"

"No," Paul said, shaking his head. "That took years. He sent me to a brother in Damascus who prayed for me, and I could see again. Then I went into the desert. I had to work it all through. I had been wrong. About everything!"

He looked intently at Linus. "Everything."

Linus waited. Perhaps he had been wrong, too.

"You can be right, in the world's eyes. Or you can walk with God. You can be right… or you can have His righteousness. But not both. Which do you want?"

Linus nodded slowly. "I want Him. I really do."

Paul turned to face him directly.

"Linus, he loves you passionately. Created you for himself, to live with him for this life and the life that never ends. When he comes, we'll be changed. We'll be like him. We are already his brothers for eternity. What Jesus did for you removes all barriers between you and the Father, between you and God."

"So, when I die, I can know him?"

"Why wait?"

"I can know him now?"

"Right now."

"Not just know about him? Not just know his ways, the things he's said, and the scriptures? Really know him?"

"Yes," said Paul. "Really know him. Now."

Linus leaned back, and then lay all the way down, flat on his back, and closed his eyes.

"Paul," said the younger man, "I believe you've killed him! Would you pass me that bread he's not going to be eating?"

"Surely!" said Paul, handing the platter over the table. "He's chewing on other things now!"

When the meat was brought, and the smell of carrots and gravy and more bread was overwhelming, Linus sat up.

"What? He lives?" they all shouted in mock surprise.

"Apparently," said Paul. "Hungry?"

"For more than food," laughed Linus. "Much more than food. But as long as it's here…"

When the laughs subsided, Paul handed him the meat platter. "Start with this, and tell us what you've decided."

"Has this meat been in the temples?" asked Linus, with a fork full halfway to his plate.

"Do you mean, has it been offered to the idols in those temples?"

"Yes. If it has, you can't eat it, can you?"

The men around the table continued cutting and eating the meat, and simply looked at him.

"All right," said Linus. "Help me understand!" He looked around the table, struggling with what he was seeing. "You are all Jews!"

"Linus," asked Paul, "will you insist on doing it right? Is the Law how you will live?"

Linus stared at him. "It's the same discussion, isn't it?"

"Exactly. You can be right in the eyes of the world, or you can let His righteousness cover you. And if you're depending on Him, then you've left all the rules about being 'righteous' behind. All the regulations about what you can touch, what you can eat and drink, where you can go … have nothing to do with the Kingdom of God. Nothing at all."

"I'm beginning to see why it took years in the desert!" smiled Linus. "I did not grow up with anything like that, but you had a life built on 'doing it right'… and He had to take you back to the beginning?"

"All the way back. His ways are not our ways. I warn you, none of it makes sense to your rational mind. It's a life based on His ways, not ours. Weak is strong, first is last, foolish is wise. The king is a servant. Death brings life."

Linus shook his head. "Is it worth it?"

"What? Giving up everything you thought you knew … giving up your life itself, to have His life instead? To know … Him?"

"Yes."

Paul leaned back and laughed, and laughed some more, and the others joined in around the table. Finally he responded, wiping his eyes. "Forgive me, please. Yes. Yes, and again I assure you, yes!"

Fourteen

Julia awoke to realize Gadol was sitting in the opening of the cave, watching her.

She sat up, leaned against the wall, and waited.

"You first," she finally said, as his yellow eyes stared, and he said nothing.

"They despise you, you know that."

"That's ridiculous," she retorted. "What are you doing?"

"It's true. I've heard them talk."

She decided to ignore this line of conversation.

"Why did you bring me here?"

Gadol pushed back from the ledge, and coasted off into the morning sun.

Feeling the hunger of too much time with no food, she walked to the opening. To her surprise, there was a bit of fruit lying there, several pieces that looked something like bananas. She opened one: it was fresh, sweet, satisfying. Quickly she ate all of them, and threw the skins out into the ravine below.

Settling down against the wall, she raised her arms, palms up, and began singing an old, favorite psalm. Closing her eyes, she imagined herself to be Home, with the one who had redeemed her. She could see his face, feel his warm hand on hers.

"What should I do?" she murmured. "I have no idea what's going on."

"Are you afraid?" he asked, deep within her.

She thought a moment.

"No."

"You know my love for you."

"Yes."

And he began singing the psalm she had just begun. Smiling, she sang with him, and when the song finished she was alone again, watching the sun rise higher into the eastern sky over those incredible mountains.

"No," she whispered, "I am not afraid."

Job also headed out across the plains, but north and east to strike the range much further to the north than Julia's path. In three days he was climbing rough foothills into a high range, with pines towering above him and a deep silence all around.

As he climbed, the air became cool, and he felt more need to breathe deeply and rest more often. A soldier, a farmer, a traveler, he had always been in excellent shape, and the new body was almost indefatigable, but this was strenuous.

On a slope facing west, perhaps five thousand feet above the plains running to the distant horizon, he found a ledge that offered level ground and put his pack down. He opened the laces to pull out two apples and a melon, and settled down to watch the sunset. Both of them.

As the night swallowed up the last red and orange streaks on the horizon, the stars easily outnumbered the sand on all the beaches there ever were. It was hard to choose the brightest ones, among such a thickly splattered canvas. He thought of proposing some constellations for this new planet, but choosing primary stars was beyond him in the blazing scenario above.

I must be looking into the galaxy, from the edge…

He stared deep into the heavens. He looked closer at one section, and, as Julia had done, discovered he could see further, the more he focused. Intently probing one of the densest regions of the star field, he looked between the points of light, and chose something that looked a bit fuzzy. Closer and closer he peered, and a galaxy far beyond his own came into a clear picture. He could now see its shape. He chose a star in that galaxy, and focused on it until it was absolutely clear. He found a planet around it, and soon knew the basic geography of that world.

Leaning back, he closed his eyes to rest.

"Astounding…" he murmured.

A thought occurred to him. If they could see distance so well …

When dawn's chill presence eased over the eastern slope behind him, he rolled over on his pad to study a flower just in front of his face. Looking closer, the veins of the petals were plain to see. He stared more intently, and the structure of the leaf became clear, and looking ever more closely, he was soon examining the cellular structure of the leaf in all its complexity.

"You are pleased with His handiwork?"

The silvery voice startled him, and he looked over his shoulder to see a Watcher standing behind him. The increased brightness was not the sun emerging from the peaks, as he had assumed.

Job rolled over and sat up.

"Welcome. You arrived quietly."

"My apologies, I did not wish to interrupt. I am 'Athelkan."

"You are one of the Sons of God, as is 'Athaq?"

"Indeed."

"But 'Athaq has responsibility for this region … doesn't he?"

"Yes."

"Do you travel in each others' domains?"

"Occasionally."

'Athelkan waited.

"May I help you?" asked Job, finally.

"We have not gotten acquainted, since you arrived. I remember you well from the time of your trial, of course. But you do not know us."

Job smiled. "How much of my difficulties were you aware of? It seemed very private to me, at the time."

"The universe watched," 'Athelkan replied simply.

Job shook his head.

"We listened to every question. Every cry. Every moan."

"Why?"

'Athelkan was quiet for a while, then responded, "The One offered your faithfulness as proof for all to see. Proof that men could love the Creator for Himself, not just because of what He did for them. It was the purpose for which he made Adam, and all of Adam's children."

"To be loved by Him, and to love Him in return," whispered Job.

"That's what it has been about, from the beginning."

"Lucifer challenged Him about that. The One trusted you to be His evidence, the proof that He was right. For all of Creation to see."

"What did you expect? You, 'the sons of God' who watched?"

'Athelkan's expression was unreadable. Finally he answered.

"The challenge surprised us. The response, His offer of your suffering surprised us even more. We had no basis to form expectations."

"Because you did not know Adam's race? Did not know how they … how we … how I might respond?"

"Comfort seems very important to the once-born," 'Athelkan replied with a small smile, and said no more.

"Indeed," agreed Job. "Indeed. And I had my share. I was greatly blessed. So you did not know whether I would choose comfort … or faithfulness."

'Athelkan shook his head. "We did not. And the counsel of your friends confused us."

Job laughed. He thought about it for a while, then laughed again, and when he could not stop, lay down on the ground and chuckled for a while.

"Excuse me, please, 'Athelkan. Excuse me."

'Athelkan waited, silent and motionless.

Job breathed steadily for a minute, wiped his eyes, and sat up.

"They confused me too, let me just say that!"

"Apparently the One was not impressed."

"No, apparently not!" Job laughed again, and chuckled for a minute. "But He forgave them!"

"Only because you did."

"Mmm. You think so?"

They were quiet for a moment, and Job looked out over the western landscape, glowing in the morning light. The sea shone in the far distance, not quite to the horizon from this height.

"Tell me …" 'Athelkan finally spoke.

Job waited.

"He spoke to you of the 'cords of Orion'…"

Job did not respond.

"Did you know … did you have any idea what He meant?"

"Certainly not. We spoke in my time of Orion's belt in various ways, but what it meant to 'loose' the 'cords' … I had no idea."

Remembering back, he added, "I was so overwhelmed by His demonstration of Lordship, of sovereignty -- of the distance between the Creator and my wretched self -- it was one of many things that simply swept me into shame over my words."

"And now?"

"You mean, do I yet understand what they are?"

"Yes."

"Do you?"

'Athelkan did not respond, and Job waited. The question was never far from his thoughts, and if one of the shepherds of the universe wished to discuss it, he intended to listen, not talk.

For several minutes they were silent. The second sun had risen above the peaks behind Job now, and the view to the west was brilliantly lit.

Finally Job spoke. "That question is always in my mind, 'Athelkan, and He told me little before we came. If you can offer any understanding, please do so."

"I have a thought. No more."

"Yes?"

"There are paths … between the stars."

"Paths?"

"Do you understand light?"

Job shook his head. "I've heard people talk, people who lived far later than I did, of waves and particles, as though light can be both water and a stone. That it can spread like ripples, and bounce like a pebble. And then, in Heaven, the Light is verily alive! How can that ever be understood? No, I do not understand it!"

'Athelkan smiled. "You feel the heat from the stars, from the suns, and they smite you with their brilliance."

"Yes, certainly."

"Can you see within them, Job? I have wondered."

Job grinned. "You struggle to understand Man's experience of the universe, and even more, twice-born Man's experience!"

'Athelkan smiled again. "I do. It is surpassingly difficult for us. What you feel, what you think, how you reason … all are a mystery. And then … to be made in the image of the One. It is to me as Light is to you, beyond comprehension!"

"Yes," answered Job, after a moment, "I am discovering that I can see within them. There seems no limit to what my eyes can see, whether far, or deep, or small. I was just beginning to explore that, when you came. And I am wondering about the other senses we have. Hearing, smell, touch… I wonder …"

"Indeed," mused 'Athelkan. "As you explore that, please speak to me about it."

"So," said Job. "You were saying, about Light. Yes, I feel the heat, I see the brightness. And?"

"What you see, what you feel, has come to you from the star. It throws its energy to the Universe, constantly, in all directions."

Job nodded. And waited.

"Other stars are doing the same."

"Yes," said Job, struggling to see where this might go.

"Those emanations meet. They cross. They build upon one another, in ways that once-born man could not have imagined."

"And therefore could not rationally understand."

"Yes, I suppose that is true."

Job pursed his lips, and nodded. "Tell me … when the stars combine their radiance … when those 'emanations' meet … what happens?"

"It becomes tangible. To the spirit beings, it is … available."

Job thought. Had he been aware of them, and not realized what he was sensing?

"Available, as in … like a road, or a rope?"

"Yes, in a way. As pathways."

"How are they used? By whom? How much? What do they … what do they do?"

Now 'Athelkan laughed, and Job stared. The silvery sound and its rich overtones delighted him.

"'Athelkan, your voice is beautiful. Do you, do your 'brothers' … sing?"

"Of course! Did you think that special delight would be kept only for Adam's children?"

"I suppose not, I suppose not." He smiled at himself, shaking his head. Would the obvious always be so mysterious? Would the mysterious always turn out to be so obvious?

"All manner of creatures use the pathways to travel among the stars. For those who are spirit - not flesh - it is a common way, a common … transport, you would say."

"To move through the heavens … from star to star?"

"Every star shines at every star."

Job frowned, his mind racing. "There's light … everywhere!"

"Yes."

"Do they travel on these pathways at the speed that light moves?"

"Do you know what that is?" laughed 'Athelkan.

"No, but … some do!"

"Yes, you're right. Some do. Let me ask you a question in return: on Earth, did you move with your roadways? Did you travel at the speed your roadways moved?"

"No, much faster. We moved on them, not with them! They did not move at all!"

'Athelkan smiled. "It is the same with us, with our pathways."

Job rubbed his eyes. How fast was that? If "fast" even made sense, to spirit beings in eternity…

A sobering thought occurred to him. A thought that opened unexpected possibilities. "Do you think Leviathan's kin could use these? Being flesh, now?"

'Athelkan nodded. "That is a concern in my mind. I have been thinking on it. I do not see how they could survive the use, if so … for flesh, the attempt should be fatal. But having been spirit, they know the pathways well, and might try."

Job frowned. "Could we use them? We are flesh, but Spirit-born as well…"

'Athelkan stared at him. "Would you need to?"

Job studied his face, trying to read his thought, but 'Athelkan said no more.

"Then, you believe these are the 'cords'?"

"I have no other suggestion."

After a moment of silence between them, 'Athelkan said, "I will leave you now. Again, welcome to Orion."

Suddenly Job was alone, and the brightness of dual suns seemed suddenly dimmer that it was before.

He lay back and thought for a while. Were the Watchers probing him? Was the request for more understanding of twice-born man's condition only what it sounded like, only the curiosity that the angels share?

"I can't read the mind of man, how can I know the mind of a Watcher?" He shook his head.

But the promise. That we would know, as we are known. Did that just apply to our relationship with the Son? Or with all the sons of Adam … surely so.

Yes, he decided, he was comfortable in his complete discernment of the team that traveled with him. Hadn't thought about it, but it was clear. He knew them, he really did, deeply and completely.

Well, then, why not others? Why not trust his discernment of Watchers, and Leviathan's kin, and the animals and the sea life that was emerging here?

"I need to pay more attention to that," he muttered. "It's important."

It was two days before Gadol returned. At dusk, he landed on the cave floor and settled down, filling the entrance. On the ground before him were two large melons and more of the bananas, bruised by his claws.

Julia stood and stretched, pressing her hands against the ceiling of the cave to feel her muscles tense and strain against the resistance. Without speaking to him, she walked up to the beast, picked up the fruit, turned away, and walked back to the depths of the cave. She sat behind a turn in the rock where he could not see her, and began to peel a banana.

"Hungry?" growled Gadol.

"Not any more."

"They despise you. You know that."

She did not bother to answer.

"Why did you come here?"

"For the pleasure of your company, of course."

He snorted. "You had no idea I was here."

"You're right. So, tell me. Why are you here?"

A low rumble shook the air, and the cave heated up noticeable. Julia smiled. She stood, took one of the melons out into the open area of the cave where Gadol could see her, and broke it open on a sharp turn of the cliff wall. She picked up the pieces, slowly and carefully, not looking at him at all, and walked back out of sight to continue eating.

"So," she repeated, "why are you here?"

"My father …"

"Is Leviathan. Yes. I asked why you are here. I know where he is, and I know why he's there."

Gadol growled and stood up. "Not your concern." He pushed off from the cave entrance, and in a whoosh was gone.

Julia smiled again, and broke open another melon. Not too bad, she thought, just the right sweetness.

In the dark between midnight and dawn the scrape of rock and a sudden blast of wind told her he was back. Without moving from her warm spot deep in the cave, she mumbled, "Yes? Have you decided to answer my question?"

"We will go now."

"I'm sleeping."

"Do you want to stay here forever?"

"I'm beginning to like my cave. I was thinking of where to put the furniture."

Gadol roared in frustration, and Julia buried her head as the steam and flame swept into the small space.

"Is that why you're here? Because you have a temper?"

A long silence followed, and she waited.

"My father rebelled."

"The One does not hold you responsible for that. You are not here because of him. What did you do?"

Again, silence.

"You can return to Him, you know. You can turn from your anger, your hatred. He forgives, just as He heals."

Gadol's breathing became noisy and strained. Julia decided she had said enough for the present.

"Are there others? Do you have brothers?" She decided she didn't want to know if he had sisters.

"Yes."

"Where are they?"

"Scattered. Prisoners."

After a moment, he continued, "Like me." A bitterness saturated his voice.

"Can you talk to them?"

A long pause ensued.

"At times."

So this was a secret. Why would he tell her that? He shook noisily, and a low rumble vibrated the night. Maybe he hadn't meant to.

"Have any of them turned back, turned to the One?"

"We are all … faithful." The last word was so strained Gadol almost choked on it. Julia laughed, as quietly as she could. When she could trust her voice to be steady again, she changed the subject.

"Good. I'm so glad to hear that. What can I do for you?"

"It is time to return?"

"To … the others?"

"Yes."

"Those men who despise me?"

"Yes."

He waited too long to answer me, she thought. He's not sure what I think.

"Can I trust you?"

He hesitated again.

"I will take you where they are."

She thought about that. He meant what he was not saying, obviously, but what he was saying was true. Deathly tired of the cave, she made up her mind.

"All right. I trust you."

Gadol stared, as she came out from the back of the cave and stretched before the long ride.

It occurred to her that no one trusted him, no one ever had. No one ever had any reason to trust him. Her statement of trust confused him. She turned away for a moment, looking back into the cave, to hide the smile. The she came and stood before him.

"Can I ride this time, or must you carry me like a dead thing?"

Gadol turned, offering his side and back for her to climb on. She had ridden a few times already, so knew where to step and what to hold. In a minute, she was settled.

Gadol took three steps into nothing. The black of a moonless night surrounded them, and a cover of cloud hid the stars. His wings beat steadily, and he turned until she did not know the direction they flew. They climbed higher, and the air chilled. She clung tightly to him, having no ropes to secure her nor pads to soften the perch. Her knees quickly scraped raw, and her palms would be bleeding soon. On they flew.

A wave of heat flowed over her, and Julia awoke with no idea where she was. Dawn was breaking, her body was so stiff it might never move again, and she was clinging to a rocky ridge. No, a dragon's back. Flying. The sight of stormy waves just fifty feet below brought it back in a rush. They seemed to be flying straight towards a cliff face.

Gripping the rough skin and bony ridge of his backbone even tighter, she screamed into the wind, "Where are we?"

The answer did not help. "Hold on. Get some air!"

With that, he turned into a dive and they fell straight down, his wings pinning her to his side. Almost forgetting the part about taking a breath, she hid her face in the sweaty hide, and waited.

They crashed into the cold water a hundred feet from the cliff, and did not return to the surface. Julia held her breath, and held it, and held it, and despaired of being able to hold it another second.

They broke the surface.

Absolute darkness and silence greeted them. Gadol eased up against a rock and she carefully unfolded her aching body from its death grip on his back. When she was able to shift her weight to the rock and drag her bruised body up to the top, a gurgle told him he had gone back underwater, and she was alone.

Trying to stand, she found that one leg would not hold her weight, and she was desperately weak.

"Hello?"

Her trembling voice echoed in every direction. Where was she?

"Hello?" she shouted, but there was no response.

Feeling about the top of the rock, she almost fell off. Smaller across than she was tall, it offered little room to lie down, much less walk. She felt for something to throw, and found some fragments of rock. At least, she hoped it was rock. Picking a direction at random, she threw it, and heard it splash. Turning around, she threw at what seemed to be the four points of a compass, and heard a splash in three directions; the fourth clattered onto rocky ground.

She knelt to feel of the rock she was on, and find a marker that would indicate that direction. At the edge there was a rough pattern that she might be able to recognize again. How far was it?

"It doesn't matter. You can't walk, much less swim!" she muttered.

The sting of the salt water on her hands and knees was fading, and there was nothing she could do about those wounds anyway. She curled up, and was quickly asleep.

Fifteen

John made his way back to the coast, and climbed down the gravel ravine to the rocky shore. Were there fish close by? Surely so.

"Can you hear me?" he called out, across the surf.

"I don't even know who I'm calling, or what," he laughed, as he waded out knee-deep into the breaking waves. The ocean floor dropped quickly away here, and he could feel the waves pulling at him under the surface.

He noticed a rock offshore that he hadn't seen before, and studied it. Slightly rounded, it looked smooth, but with a pattern … and it was moving!

The "rock" drifted in with the waves, and washed up to the surf in front of him. Eight feet across, dark green and brown, it suddenly stabilized. And stood up.

The massive sea turtle gripped the sand and rock beneath its feet and moved slowly in, finally stopping squarely before John. He squatted down, and looked at its eyes.

A thought occurred to him. "Did you come because I called?"

The turtle lifted a right front leg and claw, and made a step closer to him. Then it looked up at him.

"Can you take me out there?" John pointed to the rolling waves beyond them.

The turtle slowly lifted great padded claws, turned, and stood facing the sea.

"All right, then!"

As he climbed on, he muttered, "I wonder if I can swim…"

Once he was settled, or as settled as he could get on a wet, rocking surface that was only occasionally above the water, he tapped the shell a couple of times. The turtle pushed on the sand with his claws and great arms, and floated into the breaking waves. They rode up and down over the first two waves as they curled and broke, then were past them and riding on the deep swells of the open sea.

The turtle moved away from the cliffs that had become so familiar, they were quickly out into the blue-green expanse. It paused, as though asking for direction. John tapped on the left side, and the great creature turned south. The waves now rolled past from John's right to his left, rocking in a new direction.

"Thank you," he called out. "I've never been on the sea before, and certainly never with a turtle!"

He felt the turtle was pleased, somehow. Could he communicate with it in some way? How did Job communicate with Gadol, before speech began between them? But Gadol was a spirit-being, constrained in flesh. That was different, surely.

"Tell me about yourself," he ventured.

In his mind, images began forming. They seemed distorted, and cast in shades of green and grey, with occasional yellows and reds that were strangely muted. A great structure of intricately carved material loomed before him, and colorful things were fastened to it … growing on it? Above, there was a bright light shining, but as though it were on the other side of … of water?

With a shock, he realized he was seeing the turtle's world, as the turtle saw it, from some distance below the surface. And his eyes did not join what each saw into a single image, as human eyes do, so distortion was the effect of that difference.

The view turned, and several small turtles came into view. They swam up to him, and seemed to bump into his face, in the image in his mind.

"Oh!"

It startled him so much, his attention came back to the sea and the turtle under him. The image vanished.

After a moment, there seemed to be a question in the air. A request. For him to share his own background?

He had nothing to offer, from earthly life. But no, he did remember some things. He too had lived in water, held in the warmth of his mother's body. He remembered sounds, music, voices. He offered those images to the turtle, and somehow felt it was being received.

In his memory, the image changed to a time of great stress and emotion, then excruciating pain. He stopped, bringing his mind back to the present day. He did not want to share that with the turtle; how could he explain it?

The turtle stopped swimming, and the emotion John felt from it was grief, a deep, empathetic grief. Did the creature understand?

Apparently so.

John then turned his mind to heaven, and when he arrived to meet Jesus. Suddenly a fascinated interest surrounded him, and he could tell the turtle wanted to know more.

"Here's what he looks like," said John aloud, and brought Jesus to his mind. Great pleasure seemed to emanate from the creature below him. John allowed himself to sink back into that memory.

"Welcome, John. Welcome to the love of Father, and the life you were created for, the life with your Father."

"Where am I"?

"You have died, and your life on Earth is ended. You have come Home."

"Was it time? Did something go wrong? I don't remember anything outside of … the place I was."

"Your mother was afraid, and your father was busy. They decided not to let you be born. Now you are here. Home. With me. With Father."

John looked about. Then he looked at himself.

"I'm changed. I wasn't like this … moments ago!"

"You're full-grown. In the womb, you were a baby."

"Will I stay like this?"

Jesus laughed. "For ever!"

John looked at Him.

"I've never seen you before, but I know you. Were you with me … in there?"

"Yes, from the beginning."

"Yes. It's true, I see it now. Thank you."

"Come with me, to the home I've prepared for you. And to meet Father, for you already know Him, too."

Job packed up his bedroll, pulled the wide-brimmed hat down to his eyebrows, and turned east up the slope. Picking his way through rock and gravel, he came to smooth grass and scattered pine, thinning out as he climbed.

Suddenly there were no more trees, and the grass gave way to bare rock that would be covered in snow in the winter. A gap through the high ridge before him opened up to the right, and he headed that way. An hour later he emerged onto the pass between the higher peaks, and looked over another range of peaks, rising higher than the one on which he stood.

Starting down the far side, he found the slope was smooth and he traveled fast. Soon the trees began, and deep grass under them, and as he walked deeper into the woods the tops of the trees joined and blocked most of the light.

A small herd of deer were suddenly in front of him, looking up in surprise at the newcomer.

"Hello!"

The buck began walking towards him, and the others followed. A beautiful doe and two wobbly fawns, freckled over their backs and sides and nudging up against mama as they walked.

"Congratulations," said Job to the buck, "your family is beautiful."

The buck lowered his head for a moment, then came closer, pushing his nose into Job's chest and then stepping back. Job reached out to stroke his face, lightly tracing the line from above his eyes down his nose.

"Do you have a name yet?"

The buck offered no response, and the doe moved up close beside him, as though she were joining the conversation. She leaned gently into her mate's side. Job smiled.

"How about 'Faithful', and for you, my lady, 'Beloved'?"

The buck turned, looking at the doe, and she returned the gaze for a moment. He then looked back at Job and bowed his head again.

"Excellent. When the fawns are ready for a name, we would be glad to suggest something."

They both bowed and backed away, then turned and moved off into the trees, nuzzling the ground to find whatever the trees had dropped for them. The fawns stayed as the doe moved away, leaning into each other and looking at Job. He knelt down, and they staggered to him. He pulled them close, running a hand down their backs, and they nuzzled into his shoulders and chest.

"I think we'll know each other for a long time," Job said quietly. "Come see me when you're older!"

When he finally moved on down the slope, leaving the fawns trailing after mom and dad, he quickly came to a level shelf on the mountainside. It opened to the north, with a lawn that could have been kept by a gardener, spreading out fifty yards wide and hundreds of yards along the face of the slope. At the far end stood a tree, majestic and perfectly formed. How could it have grown so fine, so fast? An oak? Sweet gum? Maple? What could it be?

Unconsciously, he took off his hat, though the larger sun was directly over him, and the day as bright as any he had seen here. He walked a few steps toward the tree, and suddenly sat down to unlace and remove his boots. And his socks. Standing again, carrying hat in one hand and boots in the other, he walked barefoot down the center of the lawn, straight to the tree that drew him as surely as a mother calling her child.

It towered over him as he approached, and the fruit on its lower branches was fragrant and golden. A stream came from under its roots and wandered off to the downhill slope to the east.

He stood under the fringes of its branches, looking up into the foliage and smelling the fruit, a rich, subtle fragrance with a mild sweetness and the promise of juicy satisfaction.

But he took none, somehow could not reach for one. And the desire was not compelling, as it would have been on Earth. He realized he was free to enjoy the sight, enjoy the tree, enjoy the fragrance, and it mattered not if he left without eating … he would be just as content.

"What are you?" he asked.

"You know its name, Job. We guard one like it, in the first garden."

Turning, Job recognized what must have been one of the cherubim, though he was fairly sure they had not met. Four faces, a thirty-foot wingspan, and eyes covering the wings. Unmistakable.

"Welcome," he said with a bow, hardly knowing what else to say.

"It is I who say 'Welcome,' Job." The softly thundering voice rolled across the meadow. "Do you enjoy it?"

Job turned back to the tree, and looked up the height to the top. "I've not seen one like it. Magnificent."

"The fruit is yours to eat, if you like."

"In the first garden, there was another tree close by, and its fruit was more troublesome," said Job. "Surely this one is like the Tree of Life, and not the other!"

"Indeed," responded the cherubim. "The life in this tree, and the life in you, are from the same source."

"Why was the fruit of the other tree so deadly?" mused Job. Turning to the cherubim, he said, "Can you say?"

"Two things, I believe."

Job savored the aroma of the tree and the fruit, waiting for him to continue.

"To take of it was the first Rebellion, and opened the door for the evil one to establish his throne in the heart of Adam."

He was quiet again, looking at the tree.

"But it was also a choice to lust after righteousness apart from the One … to reject Him as Righteousness itself … and choose something else."

"But there would be no place in Heaven, or the Creation, for a life outside Father's dominion. It could not exist!"

"So it is. Therefore the choice was … a choice to die. To have no place. To no longer exist."

"Indeed. Indeed. Without the righteousness from him, we would have no place."

"And the second Adam took back the title deed, as well, that the first had given away. So you have both Righteousness and Dominion. All is restored, and more so!"

"Yes, more so. A place on the throne, not just 'below the angels.' Well said."

They looked back at the tree, and Job took a deep breath.

"I have wondered," he said. "Was the guard placed to keep Adam and his family from returning to the garden, lest they should …"

"No, not at all!" exclaimed the winged spirit. "It was to keep the way open!"

Job stared at him.

"We were guarding the way, not blocking it. Did you not read what was written?"

In the gathering dusk, Job stepped from the long, smooth lawn down onto the slopes leading to the deep valley between the ranges. As night fell, he reached the edge of a cold, fast stream running across his path towards the south. A space opened between the trees and the stream where a man could lie and watch the stars move across the heavens; the first moon was up, and the second would soon follow.

He was studying the two moons an hour later when a shape moved across the first one, and then completely covered both of them. The shape took on an outline, and then the unmistakable sound of the rough wings of Gadol, or something like him. A moment later, it landed between Job and the stream.

"You are not Gadol," said Job. "You smell different."

"And you stink to me," it replied.

Another creature landed just behind him; moments later, a third that looked somehow more familiar.

"Ah, Gadol. You are just in time to introduce me to your … friends. Brothers?"

Gadol snorted, and began to speak.

"Shut up."

Another creature dropped from the sky, a smaller one. As it landed, it seemed to stumble, and it stayed well back from the others.

Job's eyes had adjusted from looking at the moon, and could tell the one in front was much bigger than Gadol; no colors or features were visible in the dark, looking at them with bright moons behind them. The largest had spoken.

"You are Job," it said, with raw contempt in its voice. "You had your chance to curse God and die. You should have taken it. Now you belong to me."

Job sat silently, looking to the Father in his spirit, waiting to see what he should do or say. Nothing came to mind, so he waited.

"When do you finish here, and leave?"

He sat silent.

"Where do you go next?"

He waited.

The creature swept a claw into the ground and threw enough dirt and grass onto Job that he was instantly buried. He pushed it off him, and slowly climbed out of the mound. He sat down on top of it, brushing debris from his hair and shoulders.

"How did your friends get here?" he asked, picking up the conversation as calmly as he could.

"It doesn't matter."

"That's not allowed, is it?"

A snort, nothing more.

"Did you use the light … 'pathways'?"

The creature in front exploded. "Did you tell him?" he demanded, turning on Gadol. "Have you no brain at all?" A full backhand sweep of that massive claw smashed into Gadol and threw him into the stream, rolling and splashing across it to the far side.

Gadol slowly stood up, and did not move from where he stood. Job could read no expression on his shadowed face, but knowing that Gadol was not guilty of the charge, he imagined the raging, self-righteous fury inside the smaller animal.

"Did your father never teach you any manners?" asked Job, quietly.

"I am Livya-Tontal, of the planet 'Nsela at Mintaka, son of Leviathan. I need no manners."

"I am Job, and I have dominion on 'Nsol. Does 'Athelkan know you are here?"

"He told you of the light paths!" roared Tontal.

"Yes," said Job quietly.

"Did he also tell you it was impossible, and forbidden?"

"Yes."

"So you see, he is a liar!"

"Or you are."

Tontal stepped closer, engulfing Job in the smell of his body and putrid breath. "You, man of Earth, only have dominion here if I allow it! And I no longer allow it. I will cleanse this planet of you and your kin!"

He turned to Gadol.

"You have failed. Take this man and throw him in the sea! Where he lived, no one knew how to swim."

Gadol slowly waded across the stream and stood before Job.

"Now!" belched Tontal, and Gadol jumped. He took another step forward, launching into the air as he did, and the massive claws grabbed Job as he swept past, with no regard for how he was held.

As they flew east toward the coast, great clouds came over and around them, and what little Job could glimpse of the moons disappeared completely. The air became much colder, and rain pelted them. Hanging upside down, Job passed out, awoke, passed out, and awoke. He had no idea how high they were or how long they had flown, when Gadol suddenly released him and he toppled down through gusting winds, driving rain, and total darkness.

Sixteen

John studied the coastline. The cliffs on the left were giving way to a sloping forest that came down to the water's edge. They came to a place where the coast cut inland sharply, then back out.

"A river comes down there, from the cliffs?"

The turtle turned, and moved with the waves in to the shore. Storm clouds were building up behind them, and the sky darkened as the two suns were blocked by the dark grey masses above them.

Big drops splattered down. They swam past the breakers and into the cover of giant overhanging willows. The turtle began walking as its claws reached sand and gravel, and carried John to a jutting outcrop of turf and tree roots. He climbed off, and turned around to the turtle.

"My thanks, friend. Your name?"

John felt around in his mind for the answer, which seemed to be 'Mmeshu'.

"Thank you, Mmeshu. I will see you again."

Mmeshu backed up, turned into the waves, and slid underwater as soon as it was deep enough.

"Glad to be back under, I guess!"

John turned and walked into the forest, immediately protected from the rain that beat down on the upper branches. Large oaks interspersed with pine provided more cover, and he settled down under one with grass and moss in abundance.

When he woke, the world was dark. Hearing the pounding surf close by, he remembered where he was. What else was here?

Rustling in the grass nearby told him he was not alone.

He rolled to the side, looking in the darkness for whatever made the sound. "Come on over, whatever you are!"

The noise stopped. He waited, and held out his hand.

A light touch, almost a feather's touch, on his fingertips.

"Come on, it's all right."

Into his hand came a long slender body. It slid across his hand, and kept coming, and kept coming, along his arm and onto his chest. He lay back down, and waited, curious to see what had found him.

Finally the body was past his hand, and seemed to be collecting on his chest. It curled up there and settled in.

"Well, I'll see you in the morning, whatever you are!"

When he woke, the first sun was well up in the sky, and the second just rising. The weight on his chest was still there; he looked down to find a snake looking back. Black, except for golden diamonds along its back and a splotch of red over its eyes, it stared unblinking at him, with a questioning sort of look.

"I'm John. Do you have a name yet?"

No response.

"How about Wosa?"

The snake tilted its head, as though thinking about it. Finally the question seemed to be resolved, and it tucked its head into the curl of its body and began breathing slowly and deeply.

"Actually… Wosa? … I'm ready to get up."

Wosa raised its head, looked at John for a moment, and began to uncurl. It pushed off to the ground beside him and steadily slid into the forest undergrowth.

"You're twice as long as I am tall, I would guess!" said John, as Wosa's tail disappeared in the brush. He rose, shook off the leaves and twigs that had blown down in the storm, and looked around. The stream flowed quietly down into the bay, and the forest seemed quiet and deep.

He began walking uphill, moving silently among the trees, generally following the river. The pines gave way to more open land and a mixture of trees, including some blossoming with apple and pear.

Under a particularly large apple tree, a raccoon was picking up apples. It appeared to have trouble deciding which ones were the right ones. It could carry about three, but each time it came to another one on the ground, it tried to pick it up, dropped what it had, then picked up what it could. Each time, it ended up with three, and as it moved away, it came to another apple on the ground, and the story repeated itself.

John sat down and called to it.

"Come here, you silly creature!"

The raccoon stopped and stared. It carefully set the apples down, and walked slowly to him.

"How many do you need?"

It cocked its head, ran back, struggled a moment, and brought three apples to set before him. Then it ran back, gathered three more, and brought them. After several minutes, a pile of apples rose in front of John.

When the raccoon seemed to be finished, it came and stood next to the pile, and cocked its head again.

"Let's have one, shall we?" John took an apple off the top of the pile, and handed it to the raccoon, who took it in both paws and held it still. John took one, and the 'coon watched him without a quiver. He took a huge bite, and the juicy sweet apple melted in his mouth.

The raccoon looked back and forth between John and the apple in his hand, and finally lifted it to his mouth and bit.

"There you go!"

It began ravenously eating the apple, and quickly consumed the entire thing.

John worked on his to the core, and decided the seeds and the stem were probably best left to the earth. He scooped a bit of earth away, pressed them in, and covered them up, leaving no trace of his meal.

"Where are you trying to take these?" he asked his new friend.

The raccoon scampered away, then paused to look back before he disappeared into the trees.

"OK, OK," laughed John. "Tell you what. Pick up as many as you can, and I'll pick up as many as I can, and I'll help you!" The 'coon ran back to the pile, and with great indecision and many changes of mind, finally had three in his paws and seemed ready to go. John picked up as many as he could hold in his hands and arms and crooks of the elbows, and set off behind the creature.

They came to a great oak with a tunnel burrowed under its roots on one side, and the raccoon disappeared into the burrow. It came back out empty-handed, and stood looking at John.

"They're all yours!" he said, setting the collection onto the ground. "Except, maybe one? Or two?"

The 'coon watched intently as John set them down and selected two. He pretended to reach for a third, and the raccoon cocked its head and barked. A soft bark, a quiet, polite bark, but with no mistake, a bark. John withdrew his hand and laughed.

"Just to see if you were paying attention!" The raccoon visibly relaxed.

"Farewell, my friend. I'm sure you'll do fine with the rest of them."

As though suddenly reminded of an urgent errand, the raccoon bowed, paused just a moment, then scurried off towards the apple tree where all the apples were piled and waiting.

John decided to see the territory from a higher view, so he took up a steady pace moving uphill. The trees quickly thinned. Soon he was climbing soft ground and gravel, moving up into the foothills of the coastal range.

Climbing over rocky ground, then between boulders and scattered trees, he made his way higher onto the range. It became more difficult to find footholds, then handholds, and the air was much cooler than where he had begun on the coastal slope. The larger sun had set, and the smaller one chased it towards the horizon. He stopped to rest and looked out over the ocean at his back. A purple sky deepened above him, reaching towards the dusky blue out over the ocean, and a band of rosy pink stretched as far across the horizon as he could see.

"Beautiful," he murmured, "just beautiful."

Looking about for a place to settle for the night, he found a more level area sheltered by overhanging rock. At the back of the sheltered area a bighorn sheep had settled in, with a lamb curled up between its hooves.

"May I join you?" he asked, moving slowly onto the shelf. The sheep lowered its head onto its front legs and watched him. The lamb slept undisturbed.

John settled with his back against the mountainside, facing out, watching the last of the sunset throw red and purple rays across the heavens. The remaining visible bit of the sun brushed the wave tops with crimson flame for a few minutes, then the world faded into grays and deep blues, with millions of stars emerging to dance in the infinite black sky above him.

"Do you have more family?" he asked the sheep, idly, feeling the need to somehow be sociable. An image of another sheep, smaller, floated into his mind, and he smiled. How much they must have missed on Earth, those who lived there, not having this ability to communicate with the world they had dominion over. Except for the part about having dominion, of course. Adam had given that away so soon. So soon.

"Is there water close by?" he asked.

The sheep slowly extricated himself from the lamb, leaving it sleeping there, and walked to the edge of the level place, looking back. John stood up; the sheep turned away and walked out onto the slope. As it crossed among the boulders, John struggled to follow, holding to boulders where possible, and sliding until he could find a handhold elsewhere. As he caught himself on hands and knees and managed to stop a slide, the sheep was beside him, standing close as though waiting.

"Can you carry me? It's too steep for me!"

The bighorn knelt down, front and back, and waited.

"That looks like an invitation. Here I come!" Slowly he reached out to get a grip in the thick white wool, and steadied himself. He stood, and pulled himself against the sheep, and raised one leg and set it over its back. When he was settled, he said, "I'm ready."

The sheep stood without apparent effort, turned, and began walking straight uphill. "How do you do that?" exclaimed John, gripping tightly to the wool behind the ram's head. The pleasure he sensed in the big animal made him laugh.

"Go ahead, show-off!"

The sheep snorted and began trotting, kicking gravel and bits of shale flying down the slope behind him.

Long before John was ready for the ride to end, the big animal topped the ridge and began sliding and jumping down the far side.

"I'm glad its dark and I can't see this!" said John, as the sheep slowed, turned, and walked into a tree line. The stars disappeared from overhead, and the close quiet of a night forest enveloped them. John heard rustlings, crunches, swishes, and realized he was hearing all the little night creatures going about their business in the sheltered world so dark around him.

Suddenly the ram stopped, and knelt down. John eased a leg up and swung it over, stiffly stepping away. The stream just beyond the ram was evident, as it whispered and bubbled down the slope.

"Thank you. May I call you Arjan?"

The ram lowered its big head, touching the tip of a great curling horn to the center of John's chest. It turned, and was gone into the night.

John knelt by the stream and cupped cold, fresh water to drink. Mmmm, delicious.

He stopped moving, and waited. Soon he could hear rustlings close behind him. He turned slowly and sat down, waiting for his visitors to become evident.

Early the next morning, John set out for the ridge the sheep had crossed in the dark. As he crossed an open area, the sound of wings caught his attention above. He looked up just as something like Gadol fell upon him. Before the claws caught him up into the air, he thought what he saw was bigger and black, with traces of green on its belly where Gadol was gray.

And then the breath was squeezed out of him, and he passed out.

The wind was cold on his face. Something squeezed his legs together, and something else crushed his chest. Linus woke. He struggled to open his eyes, and then wished he hadn't. The sea roared, whipped by rain, not many feet below. He twisted to look up, saw the belly of a great beast he did not recognize, and realized he was gripped in the claws of this monster.

The grip on his chest was so tight he could barely breathe, much less speak.

The animal felt him move in his claws, and looked down at him. The same kind as Gadol, Linus realized, but much bigger.

"Get some air!" it roared at him, then dove towards the sea.

Linus stared at the approaching waves rushing towards him. Just before they hit the water he sucked in as much air as he could, pulling at the claws to loosen their grip on his chest. Everything went black when he slammed sideways into the water.

He awoke, coughing violently, gasping for breath, lying on gravel in complete darkness.

He forced himself to breathe. Slowly.

My clothes are wet, but not dripping, he thought. I've been here a while.

He opened his tunic and felt his chest. Claws had ripped his skin, but not deeply. It stung a little from the salt water. Nothing to be done.

My legs are bruised. Can I walk?

He rolled over, and pushed up to hands and knees. All right, so far. Except his head still pounded, from whatever happened in the last place he'd been.

How did I get from that cavern ... something had closed the opening ... I fell ... that beast must have done it, then dragged me out of there.

Pushing up, he stood slowly, holding a hand over his head again. He touched cold stone before he had straightened up.

A small place. How big?

"Anyone here?" he shouted, and then winced at the pain in his head.

Sounded like a small room, but a bit of distant echo came back to him. Must be an opening somewhere.

He walked forward until he found a wall, then began walking to the left. He tripped over some rock, and began shuffling his feet to be sure not to fall. In ten minutes he was sure he had walked the same circle at least twice. Certain places on the wall felt familiar, the second time he came to them.

So where did the echo come from? Above?

He felt around the floor for some loose rocks. Taking a small one, he tossed it up; immediately it hit something and fell back. He walked a few more steps around the wall, and threw another one. Same thing. The fifth stone he threw hit nothing, and fell back on its own.

Moving in small steps in each direction and throwing rocks up, he mapped out a hole above him, maybe four or five feet wide, and too high to get through without something to stand on.

He searched the cave floor, on his hands and knees. Nothing but a few rocks.

He lay down. The darkness and silence were unrelenting. His eyes could only adjust to the light if there were some light.

A new thought occurred to him. This creature did not care if he lived or died, and did not mind injuring him for its casual purposes.

Could he be killed? No.

Could he?

The thought rattled around in his head for a moment, then was resolved.

"It is written," he whispered. "It is appointed to man once to die ... not twice. And we are kings and priests after the order of Melchizedek... priest forever by the power of an indestructible life..."

What was the intent of this ... thing?

He had been trapped in a cavern, then pulled out and tossed into this one ... dragged into it, through some underwater entrance?

If he and Gadol were working together, then ... Gadol's friendship was a lie. To what end?

Seventeen

Job awoke in blackness, sliding down a hill that felt like it was shifting and moving under him, then tilting over and riding up the hill again. Salty waves splashed over his face and he rolled to his side to cough out the water he just breathed in.

As he came more awake, he realized he was clutching something, riding something. He held a large flat thing, almost a board, but leathery and soft on the outside. And very slippery. A wave crashed over him, and he squeezed into the board, not breathing until it had passed.

Suddenly he realized the board he clutched — the thing he was riding on — was alive. Alive and swimming through the rough midnight seas.

"Thank … you …" he called out, next time he had breath to say it. There was no response. He clung tighter to what he now realized must be a fin, and tried to determine if he had any broken bones. His back was sore, and he was scraped up badly in places … where it held me, he realized, as memory came back.

Gadol. Tontal. And one other … smaller …

He awoke again, and the waves were smaller. He tightened his grip on the fin. Light was touching the sky ahead of them

So … so that is east … how far out did they take me?

Far enough to not come back.

He slept.

A rough bump woke him, and he was lying on a wet, grey, leathery surface, clutching a dorsal fin, in rolling swells just outside a line of surf. He slipped off, still holding the creature, until he was chest deep but felt his feet hit the sandy bottom below him. He patted the sides of his host, and again conveyed his thanks. The fin moved slowly away, with a smaller one following it, then disappeared under the water.

Jumping and paddling with the waves as they lifted him off the sea bottom, he scooped water behind him and bounced and walked until he was through the breaking waves, then neck deep, then waist deep on another sand bar, then knee deep, then, finally, on shore. The morning sun was up, just one.

He fell to the ground and lay there, warming in the light and heat of it.

Some time later, feeling rested and able to stand, he rose and looked about.

"Join me?" called a distant voice, and far up the beach there was a small campfire and a hooded figure sitting on the other side.

Wary of who else might be on this planet, he walked slowly towards the fire. The smell of cooked fish greeted him, and Jesus tossed back the cowl.

"Thought you might be hungry!"

Job ran the rest of the way, embracing the King and holding him for a moment. The two sat down, and without a word, Job began eating.

He looked up. "Thank you!" he blurted out, and paused to see the smile in return, and went back to the fish.

Suddenly he looked up again, and looked around them. It was only the two of them, and nothing else. No pack, no …

"How did you catch these?" he asked, grinning.

Jesus laughed. "I was a fisherman, you know."

"Yes, but …" Job looked around again. Was there a boat? A net? Nothing. He shook his head.

"Have you recovered from your ride?"

Job stood, felt around for bruises and such, and sat back down.

"Yes, I think so. Thank you for the raft you sent!"

"Well … he was glad to help."

Job thought about the creatures that had accosted him in the night.

"There were four of them last night."

Jesus nodded.

Job looked at him and waited, but no comment was forthcoming.

"They had help getting here, didn't they?"

Jesus nodded again, and finished the last bit of the grilled fish. He scooped sand over the small fire and remains, and leaned back.

"You will need to rescue the others."

Job's eyebrows went up. It had not occurred to him that his capture would be part of a larger assault on the team. "Of course. Where will I find them?"

"Follow the coast," Jesus said, motioning south along the beach. "You are not far from the land you know. A friend will meet you, and take you to them. Friends, actually."

He stood, and Job stood as well.

"And then?"

"And then, we will see what choices are made. Farewell, for now."

And Job was alone.

The smaller sun was on the horizon, the larger one already out of sight, when Job reached the coastline ridge that overlooked the familiar cave.

Friends? I wonder who, or what …

Looking down at the surf, he noticed something swimming in the shallow foam. Two things, as he looked more carefully. One seemed like a … a seal, perhaps … and the other much smaller, much quicker. An otter?

He looked about for a way to slide down the cliff face, and soon found a likely place with enough shrubbery on the steep slope to grab handholds where needed. Jumping, sliding, stepping around the bare rock, he quickly made his way to the shore. The sea creatures came to the shallows, and the seal had a coil of line looped around its torso. Several loops.

The otter scampered up through the ripples, his brown face and dark nose looking for all the world like a bandit mask above his lighter cheeks and throat. Wet whiskers dancing, he jumped around Job's feet, then started pushing at his ankles, pushing him out to the surf. The seal stood up in the rolling waves, rocking back and forth, as though it were waiting, as though it had feet on the sandbar, out past the breakers.

"You like water a little colder than this, don't you? And I know he does!"

The otter swam out towards the seal, and back to Job, and back towards the seal, jumping and splashing through the small surf.

"I'm coming, my friend, I'm coming!" Job jumped over a wave and ran splashing out through the next breaking whitecap. It was suddenly chest deep, and the seal disappeared underwater, then popped up in front of him, whiskers waggling, sad brown eyes staring into his. It turned, facing away from him, and the coiled line lay there waiting for his grasp.

"I'm … going to ride you? I should hold this?"

The seal wobbled a little, back and forth, holding itself upright in the water.

"All right…" He took the coil in his hands, and the seal dropped down under the waves and swam forward a few feet. Job spluttered, let go, and splashed to the surface. The seal was immediately back in front of him, facing away, with the coil waiting.

"Again?"

The seal continued to float in front of him, standing up, facing away.

"I think I'll hold my breath next time! You didn't mention that part about going underwater!"

The otter had been swimming around them; it came, nudged the coiled line out towards Job, and when he took it, began diving, coming up, diving, coming up, and each time, staying down longer.

"So, I need to practice this. All right. Let's go!"

He took the coil in both hands, and the seal went under. This time Job held on for several seconds, and the seal came to the surface, paused, and then went back under. Job grabbed some air just in time.

It was half a minute before they came back up, and Job gasped for air. The seal continued swimming, but on top of the waves, and Job rested on its back, breathing deeply. They were further out in the sea now, moving north along the coast. The seal turned in towards the coast. There was no beach here, just the cliff face rising out of the water, and they approached to within a stone's throw of the nearest one.

The otter swam close, and when Job looked at him, he dove under. Most of a minute later, he burst back out of the water, and peered at Job.

"That long?"

The otter dove back under, and Job counted off the time. Almost a minute, before the otter popped back out and clambered up on the seal's back, right in Job's face. He nuzzled Job, wet whiskers and all, then dove back in and began circling them. The seal seemed to be waiting, looking at the cliffs just ahead.

"Waiting on me, I guess. All right. So we're going in there, and the door is underwater. Caves, I suppose?" He took some deep breaths and patted the seal. "Let's go!" It dove. He grabbed the coiled line with both hands and squeezed his eyes shut.

One… two… three… He could not count, or it would seem an eternity. He tried to calm his mind, be still, and wait, as the water rushed past, the light disappeared, and the seconds creeped slowly by.

Suddenly the seal turned up and they burst into the air a moment later. He gasped, took several deep breaths, and patted the seal again.

"Thank you. I guess. For bringing me … wherever I am!" It floated still in the water, and Job slipped off into chest deep water, his feet landing on gravel and sand.

The seal turned and was gone, and in the complete blackness the water around him surged and receded, but without the sound of waves. Something bumped him, and the familiar nose and whiskers of the otter nudged him forward, up the sloping gravel into shallower water.

"Hello?" he called, and echoes returned with different delays from various directions. Nothing more.

He reached the shore, scooped up some gravel, and tossed it high. After a moment, the stones fell back to the ground with no clatter of hitting a roof above. He sat down, still recovering from the underwater trip. The otter came up and nestled next to him.

"Well." He stood, when he felt rested. "Let's go find them!" He held his hand up and asked again for the light that had been so useful. The glow returned, and he looked about. In three directions there was only blackness.

"Tunnels. Who knows how far…?"

The otter stood beside him, sniffing, then tentatively moved towards the center opening. It looked back.

"Fine with me. Let's go see what's there. Can you find your way back?"

Will I even want to come back here? he wondered, as they started into the open mouth of the tunnel.

Linus slept, and was startled awake by the sound of something smashing into the floor next to him. It shattered. Wet pieces of the missile hit his face and neck. He jumped to his feet, remembering just in time not to stand up all the way. When his head had cleared, and there was no more sound, he knelt down and felt around. Pieces of ... fruit? Melon? He picked one up, and smelled it. Seemed acceptable. He felt of it, and found a rind on one side and moist, soft texture on the other. He bit into the soft part, and liked what he tasted.

Hours later, he was drifting off again when he heard a voice. Very faint.

"Linus? Julia?"

"I'm here!" he roared up at the opening in the ceiling, then waited.

The voice was a little closer. "Don't speak!" it said. "Tap some rocks together, so I can find you."

Linus scrambled around on the ground, and found a couple of good-sized rocks. He began tapping them together, waiting a moment, tapping again.

"Good," came the voice, now easily recognized as Job's. "I'm on the way."

Moments later the familiar glow of Job's painted light showed above him, and Linus could see the shape of the hole.

"Ah, there you are!" exclaimed Job, as his hand came into view, palm glowing. Linus shielded his eyes, to let them adjust after so many hours of coal black darkness.

"Oh. Sorry." Job closed his hand, and the light was muted. "Now, how do we get you out?"

Job disappeared, then returned. "Give me your tunic."

"It's all I have on!" protested Linus.

"It's all we have to get you out!" laughed Job. "I'll tie mine and yours together into a rope, and that should be long enough that you can reach it and pull yourself up."

"Are you going to hold it?" asked Linus, as he stripped.

"No, you're too big for me to pull up, but ... I think I can tie a knot in one end, and anchor it here."

Linus tossed up the garment, and waited.

"I've tied a knot ... I think it will hold ... here ... I'm tying them together ... now, there it is, can you reach it?"

Linus reached up and touched the hanging end. "With a jump!" he answered.

"All right, then. It's ready, when you are."

Linus jumped up, grabbing the tunic as high as he could, and hung for a moment. Then he dropped to the floor. Bending over, hands on his knees, he rested a moment.

"I'm weak. Been a while since I've eaten."

"Me, too, my friend."

"I'm ready," said Linus, gathering his strength.

"I'll help when I can," Job assured him, and Linus jumped. From his first handful of cloth, he pulled up, hand over hand. Job lay down on the rock above him, and grabbed him under the arms as soon as Linus was high enough.

"All right, now," whispered Job, "come on up!"

With a great heave, and Job's help, Linus hoisted himself up onto the rock above, chest resting on the ledge, with his body still hanging into the hole. Job held his arms, keeping Linus from slipping down. After a moment's rest, Linus said, "Here I come!" and pushed up. Job grabbed him around the chest and rolled away, pulling him the rest of the way out.

They lay for a moment, resting.

"We need to be quiet," whispered Job. "We need to find the others, and get out of here before Gadol and his friends realize we're loose."

"How many are there?" asked Linus, taking one more long, deep breath.

"Four that I know of."

Quietly they stood, took apart the rope, and slipped back into their clothes.

"Come this way," motioned Job, "I think someone is over this way."

"How did you find me?" asked Linus. "Were you trapped, too?"

"Yes, they got all of us. But I found some help." He whistled low, then high. Nothing happened.

"Wait," said Job. "He's probably a good distance away."

Minutes dragged by. Finally a sea otter came waddling from the direction he had pointed.

"He found me, actually," said Job. Turning to the otter, he said, "What? You've found Julia?"

Apparently he had, and the otter quickly turned and moved off into the darkness.

"Come on," said Job, and he held a hand up high to light the way. They followed the animal as quickly as they could, not wanting to lose their guide in this maze of underground passages. The way became a tunnel, then a cavern, then narrow crevices, then a tunnel again. Suddenly the otter stopped. Job lifted his palm. They stood at the edge of a black pool, and Linus could just see Julia lying on a small rock in the middle of the water. The walls around the pool were too high for her to climb.

"Julia!" Job whispered, "We're here. Don't speak loudly, they might hear us. Are you all right?"

"Mostly," she replied, rousing and shaking herself. "Desperately hungry, and desperate to get off this rock, but well!"

"We'll see what we can do. Can you swim?"

"No. My leg."

Silence. Linus thought about this.

"My friend, can you carry her?" said Job to the otter, who sat close by. The animal struggled to the top of the wall and threw himself into the dark water, surfacing next to Julia in moments.

"What happens next?" asked Julia in a shaky voice, sliding down into the water and putting a hand on the otter's slippery back.

"Good question," mused Job. "Linus, if I hang down over the wall where I can lock arms with her, can you pull us both up?"

"I'm your man!" laughed Linus. Let's do it!"

The otter slowly brought Julia to the lowest point in the wall around the pool, and the men moved around to join them there. Job sat lay down on the wall and eased out over the water. Linus grabbed his ankles. Job scooted forward and Linus lowered him down. The otter brought Julia almost there, then must have turned, for suddenly she was in the water, frantically grabbing for the otter's neck. He slipped out of her grasp and disappeared.

"Help!" she blubbered as she came up. And up. And suddenly Linus realized the otter had swum under her, and was lifting her into the air. She fell against the wall, grabbing both of Job's arms.

"I'm here, Linus! Pull us up!" she cried.

Linus slowly lifted Job, and eased him down when his chest came past the top of the wall.

"Can I set you down and let go?" he asked.

"Yes, I can hold her for a moment," said Job.

Linus released Job and quickly grabbed Julia's forearms, lifting her easily over the wall.

She collapsed on the ground. In the silence Linus listened for any evidence of their captors' return.

But the wall was too high for the otter to jump, if it wanted to rejoin them. It seemed to call to Job, who stared intently at it for a moment. "All right", said Job. "Take care!" The otter disappeared beneath the water.

"What's happening?" Linus asked.

"He knows other entrances, and he needs food. He'll find us." He smiled. "They have to eat for hours a day, they burn so much energy. Did you know that?"

"I didn't," said Linus. But the idea of eating has some appeal…"

"Oh. Sorry I mentioned it!" chuckled Job. "Come on, let's see if we can find our way back!"

"Job?" Julia wasn't standing. "My leg."

"Oh, right!" He knelt down and held his palm's light over her. Linus could see swelling and scrapes all down her right leg.

"But it hurts up in here," she said, moving a hand up along the thigh and hip. "I can't stand on it."

After a few moments, Job looked up at Linus. "Father is not giving me anything to do here … is it for you?"

Linus stared at Job. "But you always …"

Job smiled, and waited.

All right, thought Linus. Maybe it is for me.

He knelt down, and Job stepped back, holding his palm out over Julia, lighting the scene.

"Father," Linus whispered, "help me to see, to do, what You're doing…"

A sense of the presence of the Holy Spirit grew in his mind, and became strong enough he almost looked up to see Him. But he waited, and began to understand the damage that had been done. And with the awareness came a confidence that God was indeed moving in him, and was going to act.

"Lie down," he said, looking up to meet Julia's eyes. She nodded, and lay back onto the stone. He closed his eyes, and let the image forming in his mind come clear, the image of the damage inside. He put one hand on her hip and the other on her knee, and began speaking to the tendons, the muscles, the bones. Calling them back to wholeness, declaring healing. Thanking and praising the Father, and moving his attention to each part of the leg as the Spirit led him. Watching, waiting, rejoicing silently as in his mind he saw the swelling go down, the bruising disappear, inch by inch.

The last was the hardest; something in the hip had been wrenched out of place.

"Almost done," he whispered. "Relax completely."

He felt her tense, then relax.

"Now," he said quietly to the hip, "be healed." It resisted. "Now!"

"Oh!" cried Julia, twisting suddenly under his hands, and then lying still.

He lifted his hands, leaned back, looked at her face, and waited.

Her eyes opened, then widened. She looked up at him.

"It's gone!"

Scrambling to her feet, she stretched and laughed. "It's gone, you wonderful bear, you did it!" She threw herself upon him and they fell they upon the rocky floor, laughing and hugging.

"Shh," whispered Job, but he was laughing as well. "Shall we go?"

I had been hanging upside down, tied to who knows what in total darkness, for more hours than I could think about, when I began imagining I saw that odd color of light that Job had used. I squeezed my eyes shut, then looked again. It went away, then came back. Could it be real?

"Job?" I croaked, throat so dry I could hardly make the sound.

The light stopped moving, then began getting larger.

"Job?" I said again, hardly more than a whisper.

In moments they were around me, though I hung higher than their heads.

"We've got to stop ... meeting like this!" I said, almost in tears. "So good to see you!"

"What are you hanging from?" Linus asked, staring into the darkness above.

"It's a secret," I said. "Could you go find out, for me?"

They looked at each other.

"Well," said Linus, "I'll be the bottom. Job, it looks like you're in the middle. Julia, how are you with heights?"

"Did I ever tell you," she said, as Linus hoisted Job up onto his shoulders, "about the circus tricks we did, my brothers and I?"

In seconds, she had scrambled up onto Linus' shoulders, then up Job's back and onto his shoulders, all of them using me as a support to stay vertical.

"Later," grunted Linus. "You can tell me later."

"How's it look?" asked Job.

"Dark. Can you wave some of that light my way?"

"Give me your hand," Job replied. She reached down, and as he grasped her hand with his, he painted it with light. She raised it up and looked at it.

"Now that would have been a great circus trick!" she exclaimed.

A moment later she had the answer. "His ankles seem to be just hooked into a crevice here ... I think if we lift him up just a bit, and he's willing to fall backwards ... onto that rock below him ... smashing his head and shoulders along the way ... there's no problem!"

I groaned.

"Well, if you insist," she replied, "I think we can lift you out of this and ease you to the ground. But when we do that ..."

"I think we can keep steady," said Job. "But let's do it now."

Julia took hold of my ankles, mashing them together as she got her small hands around them, and strained to lift me. I felt myself go up a few inches, then I guess my weight overcame her strength and my feet were crunched back into the crevice.

"Julia, if I can let go of your ankles, I can help lift him," said Job. "Are you steady enough?"

"I need the help. Let's go."

Job steadied himself on Linus' shoulders, and reached out, putting his hands under my upside-down shoulders.

"Ready."

She took my ankles again. "Now, and quickly!" she said. She heaved up and out, getting my feet clear of the rock, then I fell from her hands. She slipped down Job's back. He grabbed my legs coming by. Linus caught my shoulders before my head and hands reached the ground. We fell into a tumbled heap on the ragged rocks below us.

"Everyone ... OK?" gasped Job, as we untangled ourselves.

'Think so," I said. "Thank you."

"Yes, still in the same number of pieces," said Julia. "But you owe me dinner! I want catfish!"

"I'm OK," said Linus.

We lay there for a minute. When I got my breath back, I asked, "Where's John?"

"Haven't found him yet. I'm hoping my friend will."

"Your ... friend?"

"You'll see."

We got to our feet. But trying to stand was a challenge for me, and walking on my damaged ankles was even worse. I dropped to my hands and knees. "Just a minute," I said, looking up at them. "Give me ... give me a minute."

"Wait," said Julia, with a smile at Linus. "My turn. "

She turned to me. "Lie down."

We were soon moving quietly in the direction that Job thought best, and after some minutes I heard a soft bark off to our left. Job lifted his hand in that direction. At the foot of a tumbled rockslide was a sea otter, and in front of him, where he had been digging and scraping away the rubble, John's head and shoulders.

"Apparently they just buried him with a small rockslide," I said.

"John, are you awake? John!" Julia ran to him and rubbed his forehead and temples, and began massaging what she could reach of his shoulders.

"Come on, let's get him out," said Linus, and we began pulling rocks away. "Quiet," warned Job.

It took most of an hour, and we had him free. By that time he had awakened, still dazed, but without any broken bones.

"Hard to believe he could breathe, under all that," muttered Linus.

"I don't think he could," said Job.

We were silent for a while, and I was thinking about that little point. "They don't know if we can be killed. Maybe it was an experiment, a casual test to find out. They just left enough of him showing so they could find him later."

Job looked at me.

"Do you agree?" I asked.

No better reason for what they had done seemed apparent.

"Now. How do we get out?" Julia sounded like she had had enough of this place, and she was not alone.

"It's a good distance, and it's under water," said Job. "But we have friends."

Eighteen

Job gathered us into the main chamber, and looked us over. "Are all the injuries managed or healed? Linus, that bruise looks bad."

"Before you prayed for me, the pain was awful. That's gone. I guess the swelling will go down."

"Anyone else need attention?"

The soft glow from his raised palm showed everyone to be alert and waiting; no one asked for help. I wasn't ready yet for "dancing and leaping and praising God," but after Julia had put her hands on my feet and prayed, I certainly knew how that man felt!

"All right, let's get out of here. Our new friend will pull us through the tunnel, out to the open sea. You'll need to hold your breath for most of a minute, but it's much too far to swim on your own. Everyone able to do that?"

Everyone nodded. Surely we could do that, I thought.

"It will seem like forever, but just stay calm and wait it out. I've done it, and it's not bad when you know ahead of time it's going to be that long."

The seal turned around a couple of times in the water just off the shoal, and Job waded out to lift the coil of silken cord from its neck. He measured it out, found the center, and fashioned a loop at that point to fit around the seal's neck, close enough to not slip down the body. Then he ran the line out to its full length in both directions from there. He tied loops in each line at the midpoint and at the end.

"Come on in, everyone." We all waded out to the seal. I was chest deep.

"Everyone catch hold of a loop. I would suggest getting both hands through, so you're holding the line, and let the loop wrap around your wrists. I don't want you letting go before the ride is over!"

When everyone was linked in the chain, he paused to pray. "Father, we don't know what we'll find out there, but we know you're with us. Show us how to serve you. We forgive, we leave judgment to you, and we ask again your healing and the gift of repentance for any of these creatures that will accept it. Let your name be glorified in this place."

The seal moved out a little further.

"When we start, we'll go quickly, so we don't have to hold our breath any longer than necessary. So everyone get in the water, and be ready to be yanked under!"

Job slipped up onto the seal and held the loop at its neck.

"Ready?" Everyone nodded. Job patted the seal, and the light from his palm was suddenly bluish and pulsing as it went underwater. With a great thrust of its body, the seal forged ahead, and the living chain was pulled into motion. It dove, I guess to avoid smashing anyone into the hidden cliff edges underwater, so the pressure of being several feet below the surface put an additional strain onto the act of holding our breath, but everyone managed it.

When I thought I had to breathe or burst, the seal abruptly turned up, and brought everyone to the surface.

"Oooh," gasped Julia, that was close!" Linus hooked an arm around her, pulled her forward to the seal, and lifted her up onto his back. Job slipped off, and took her loop from her.

We gathered close in the rolling waves. We could see the cliffs of our dwelling and the waterfall some distance away.

"I think he'll pull us to a safe landing place," Job shouted. "Stay fastened. Float on your back, if that helps."

He tugged again on the seal, and the great animal began swimming steadily and gently north along the cliff. Half an hour later, it turned towards the shore where the cliffs were much lower. He brought everyone to a shallow area below a narrow, gravel-strewn beach.

Job took off the harness. "Thank you, my friend. His blessing on you and yours."

The seal pushed its body amazingly high out of the waves and fell into the surf, disappearing under the foamy water.

We pushed through the shallow surf to the beach. A light appeared ahead of us. At first it blinded me, but quickly my eyes adjusted and I saw someone very like a man standing there, like a man but much too big for someone born on Earth.

We walked up onto the gravel, and stood close together. I stared at this person. He seemed to be made of fire, or some molten metal that swirled and rearranged continuously, yet the overall effect was of something as solid as my own body.

Job bowed. "'Athaq, we meet once more. These are my friends." Turning to us, he explained, "We are in 'Athaq's domain; he is a Watcher of the heavenlies."

In his turn, 'Athaq bowed. "But why do you climb out of the sea?" he asked.

We looked at each other. How much to tell him?

Job obviously decided to tell all.

"We were held captive by Leviathan's kin."

'Athaq was silent, his expression unreadable. Finally he responded.

"Your words imply more than one."

"At least four," said Job. "I have seen Gadol and three others." We looked at him. I was surprised.

Again, 'Athaq was silent. The heat of his presence seemed to increase, and the brilliance radiating from him seemed to become even more intensely white, as though hotter, if that were possible.

"Do you know their names?"

Job did not, but he offered descriptions of a small one, almost black, another about Gadol's size, but light gray, and a much larger one, black with some green.

"Do you know these?" asked Job.

"Yes, unfortunately, I do," replied 'Athaq. "Although how they come to be here is a mystery, and one I shall have to unravel. It is not permitted."

"I believe they are all underground at this time," said Job. "Down the coast," he waved, "there are caves under the cliffs. They took us in through underwater cave openings, about 1000 feet this side of the waterfall."

"Were there other openings?"

"A cave at the top of the cliff has a tunnel that we believe joined into that cavern as well."

"I will close the openings," 'Athaq promised. "Are all of your people out?"

"Yes. We're all here."

"I am sorry you have been ill treated. I will do what I can," 'Athaq said, as he bowed, and then vanished.

Though it was broad daylight, I felt the sun had gone down. It was several minutes before the land seemed as bright as it had been before the sun-man appeared.

"Let's move out of here," Job suggested. "They may come looking for us."

We clambered across the rocks and began climbing the ravine that opened up before us, to a high meadow that must have been a few miles north of our cave. Long before we reached the top, a long, rumbling explosion echoed up the coastline, and slowly faded away. The ground trembled a bit, then all was still.

"My guess is, that door is closed!" said Julia, and we all smiled.

"Hope so," said Linus. "I have no desire to visit those caverns again."

When we emerged onto the high mesa looking out over the sea, Job suggested going back down the coast.

"To where those creatures are?" exclaimed Julia.

"Yes," said Job. He smiled. "You think it's too dangerous?"

"Well, yes!" she stammered. "Don't you?"

"You're thinking we can spy on them. That we're safer if we can know their plans," said John.

"Right. Exactly. But we'd have to stay out of sight. They were all inside, when we escaped. Where do you think they'll come out, if they can?"

I thought about it.

"There may only be one way; the cave on top is the only other opening we know of," I said. "I'll bet he … 'Athaq? … closed up the side of the mountain pretty solidly, and they'll retreat into the cavern. They'll try to come up that shaft, and even if he collapsed the cave on top, they'll work their way out eventually."

"There was a sunken place in the rocks above the cave entrance," said Linus. "I think Gadol used to sit up there and spy on us, pretty well hidden. If you're really set on going back into the fire, I say we hide out up there, and wait for them to show up."

"They won't expect us to be there, certainly. Hiding right under their noses might be the safest place," said John.

"All right. Everyone willing to do this?"

We all said yes, though I think everyone shared my apprehension.

Night was falling by this time, but the stars were bright enough to light our way. We walked south, picking our way among the rocks, the new growth of trees, and patches of thick ground cover just beginning to spread out and dig eager roots into any available soil.

Before dawn, we arrived at the hiding place.

Linus got a firm grip on the rock blocking our way, and hoisted himself up to the top. After a moment, he pulled himself over, and dropped into the enclosed space.

"He hasn't been here in a long time," he called back. We climbed up and slid down inside the boulders that circled the small open space. With everyone in, we moved silently to the pile of rock just over the cave entrance and settled down to sleep.

The following evening, the ground under our feet began shaking, in great convulsive shudders. A deep rumbling began, then silence and all was still. We moved away from the west wall, the one closest to the sea, deciding that those rocks were the most likely to tumble.

After about ten minutes a blast rocked the mountain, sending us all tumbling. When we could get to our feet we looked through the cracks on the south side, and I saw that the cave opening had been blown open. Job motioned for us to huddle close, squat down low, and be silent.

'Athaq paused after melting the side of the mountain to close the undersea cliff openings.

I must appear to be surprised by these events.

Making the light-path connection between Alnitak and the double-star Rigel, he was quickly on the molten surface of the larger sun some fifty light-years away.

"Welcome, friend," said 'Atheel, emerging from the core and presenting himself before 'Athaq. "May the One be praised."

"May He be praised indeed," responded 'Athaq. "Have you seen Guntel this cycle?"

"No," replied 'Atheel. "Do you need him?"

"Let us visit him. I hear that he may have left."

"Left?"

'Atheel regarded his friend for a moment, considering what this might mean. Turning, he led the way across the solar system to the large continent on the southern hemisphere of the planet 'Nra.

"He prefers an island off this shore," said 'Atheel, as they slipped through the atmosphere and dropped to the surface. Stepping onto the island, 'Atheel paused. "He's not here."

He lifted his gaze, and felt of the planet, reaching around it, into every coastal inlet, every desert cave, every frozen crevice in the ice packs.

"He's not here," he repeated.

"Then it's true. Job said he was attacked by Gadol and others like him on 'Nsol. Apparently the Dominant have arisen."

"How would they have assembled in one place?"

"That is the question. Let us go to Mintaka," said 'Athaq, "where Tontal was held. If they learned how to travel, Tontal would have taught them."

The light-paths took them across 180 light-years to Mintaka, the largest star in a multiple star system, and its eight planets. 'Athelkan guided them to 'Nsela, the fourth planet, where they searched for Tontal. Clearly he was gone as well.

"Let us go to 'Nsol and confront our wayward sons of pride," suggested 'Athelkan.

"I will go," said 'Athaq. "It is mine to do." He bowed to the others, and was gone.

'Athelkan considered that. He looked at 'Atheel, and the other replied, "Your question is in my spirit as well."

"We will see," said 'Athelkan. "We will see."

Nineteen

Tontal was angry. He barged into Ruunt, throwing him against the wall.

"You have failed again!" he roared, and lashed across the smaller creature's face with a claw. "Where are they?"

None of the others had an answer for that question. All the holding pens were empty, and no trace remained of the humans they had held captive just hours before.

Storming into the central chamber, Tontal stalked into the water. "I'm going out to look for them. You do the same, all of you. Every time you find one, kill him."

"Can you do that?" asked Guntel. "Are you sure that's possible?"

"We are about to find out! Now get out there!"

As he turned to dive into the water, an explosion rocked the cave. A surge of water swept in that filled the cavern and threw them all rolling from the pressure of the waves. Slammed around by the rushing, surging water, they crashed over and over again into each other and into the rock walls, until the force of the explosion was spent.

Tontal was furious. He had no idea what could have caused that eruption, but did not care. He swam recklessly towards the opening, and came suddenly to a wall of tumbled rock blocking the way. He realized he had no way of knowing how thick it might be. Turning back, he swam towards the shaft that went up into the surface cave, pushing the others out of his way.

The water filled the cavern to the top, and as he reached the shaft running up through the mountain, pushing his head up into a layer of air that still remained, a second explosion shook the mountain. What little light had been filtering down the shaft was suddenly gone. Massive pressure waves rocked the water, pushing them violently around within the chamber. Rock began falling down the shaft, smashing into Tontal's head and neck and closing off the shaft.

No air was now available in the cavern, and having been tossed against the walls, he had little left in his lungs. He began searching the many caverns and small openings that branched off from the main cavern, searching for a pocket of air in the total darkness. The others did the same.

After many hours, the water had receded a few feet, and Tontal decided finding air was no longer the most desperate need. Getting out took its place.

He returned to the main cavern and began tearing at the boulders filling the upward shaft. Small rocks came away in his claws. He came to one that had lodged in a narrowing place, and that would not be pried free. Backing off, he attacked it with a scorching blast that superheated it, and the rock exploded. The shower of debris was quickly gone, and he continued prying. After some hours, exhausted, he dropped out of the tunnel to float in the salt water below.

"Guntel! Get up there. Get us out of here."

Guntel scowled, and climbed into the shaft. When he had exhausted himself, he forced Gadol into duty.

After a day and a half of working, floating, working and floating, they reached the level of the cave and threw enough rock down the shaft to clear space in the horizontal tunnel. The air was stale and hot. Hungry and exhausted, they slept.

Tontal was first to awake, and was not about to let the others sleep. He pushed Gadol with a heavy rear claw, and slapped Ruunt awake. Guntel woke as well when the others roared in protest.

"We're going to blast our way out," declared Tontal. "This tunnel was made by melting, and it's one piece of rock now. We can heat it until it explodes, and then dig our way through the rock when it's done. Now!"

The largest of the sons of pride drew upon his hatred, his resentment, his pride, and focused that hot bitterness on the walls of the tunnel that now contained them. The others did the same. When the shell of melted rock exploded, the mountain shook.

After several hours of shoving rock behind them, Tontal saw the first crack of daylight through the rubble ahead. He pushed through, throwing rock behind him, not caring where it went or who it hit. He burst out into the fading daylight of the third day since they were trapped.

After emerging from the cave, Tontal turned and waited for the others to claw their way out before demanding, "Who let them out?"

Ruunt stammered. Tontal took that as an admission of guilt, and was determined to have a scapegoat, someone he could vent more anger upon than he had ever felt before. Nothing Ruunt could have said would have been an acceptable answer. "I am done with you," he roared, and charged him with a withering blast of flame, quickly followed by claws that tore flesh and ripped apart the body of the smaller creature. In moments, it was over, and Ruunt was no more.

Guntel and Gadol stared.

Tontal turned to them, slowly, with pure hell blazing in his eyes.

"Find them," he said. "And do whatever you want with them. Perhaps I have given you some ideas. And before you go, swear to me that they will die before either of you leave this planet."

He stepped up to Guntel. "Now."

Guntel bowed his head before the towering menace and hated glare of Tontal. "Agree."

"And you, worm?"

Gadol was half his size, and disliked being held in contempt more than Tontal could have known. Cold fury ran in his veins as he made the required promise, and the oath that followed it was not audible.

"So."

The word boomed across the mountains, and the light that accompanied it was blinding. "You have come to my planet."

The Watcher stood before them, a towering white-hot figure, holding them transfixed before him.

"And you have killed one of your own."

There was no question in Tontal's mind who was meant by "you". He growled. "Leave us, Watcher. We have work to do."

"What is your 'work'?"

No answer.

"Very well, I think I read your intent clearly enough. On with your 'work', and we will talk when you have finished."

He was gone, and to Tontal the daylight seemed as midnight for a time.

Tontal took a deep breath and turned to the others.

"Now, we hunt. Hunt and kill."

Tontal threw himself into the air towards the ocean and dove into the waves past the breakers.

Eating, thought Guntel. Not a bad idea.

Gadol stood next to him, staring at Ruunt's body, or what was left of it. Guntel looked as well, and shuddered.

"He was immortal."

Gadol turned and looked at him without expression, then looked back at Ruunt. "We need to find them, and be done with them, or we ..."

The unspoken conclusion hung in the air. After a moment, Gadol turned again and leapt into the air towards the south, staying low over the cliffs.

I have to hunt, thought Guntel. But I don't have to find.

He stepped into the evening sky, and flew directly away from the ocean.

And I can eat whatever I want.

He flew low over the grassy plains, then coasted up over the first mountain range and down into the valley. The last light of day was fading into deep purple dusk, and a moon was rising ahead of him. A lake appeared below him, reflecting dancing stars by the thousands and the colors of a red and white stone formation across the lake.

Hunger rumbled through his belly, and thirst suddenly burned as well. He fell out of the sky into the lake with an enormous, satisfying splash. Cool and refreshed and full, he emerged minutes later and took to the air again, coasting to the south in the depths of the valley, hidden from any eyes outside of the range. Thick forest covered the rising ground on both sides as he put miles of the fertile countryside between himself and everyone else.

When the two moons had long since set and dawn began coloring the sky, he had passed well out of the mountains, crossed wide plains with herds of beasts both large and small, and was beginning to feel comfortable that he would not be found anytime soon. He coasted down into a grove of trees with a variety of colors and types of foliage and found fruit to eat, fruit not unlike that in Heaven. Not so unlike. After the time in exile, this was close enough to those delights he would never taste again.

The thought stopped him as he reached for a round yellow melon hanging low on the next tree.

Never mind Tontal. What of the One?

His heart stopped.

He had been exiled to 'Nra, then brought here by an outlaw Watcher, surely in violation of His command … and sworn to the murder of Adam's children, those passionately loved by the One.

And if he ignored Tontal, his own immortality would be ended as surely as that of Ruunt.

He could not hide forever.

He looked up. The brilliant blue of the morning sky mocked him, the heavens just beyond that blue sky mocked him, and the rising heat of the first sun sought his face and mocked him.

There was no going back. He would die here, either way. Once immortal, he would now die. Soon.

He cast himself into the deepest shade of the grove, and fell into a sleep of self-hatred and black, hopeless despair.

Twenty

As the creatures stormed off in every direction, sworn to destroy us, and the brilliant light of the Watcher's presence disappeared, Job looked around. Hidden in deep shadow, I had seen nothing of what had just happened, but the noise of their confrontation was deafening.

"That was 'Athaq," said Job, "the Watcher we met earlier. Strange. He did not seem to know we were here!"

"That was my doing," said a new voice, and I looked to see Jesus standing just outside our small circle in the hiding place.

"Welcome!" said Job, and we all stood to greet Him.

"Come," said Linus, "sit with us. Let us talk."

"Gladly," He replied, with a laugh. "We won't be disturbed for a while. As you thought, your new friends will not think to look here!"

We settled down. I was delighted to have Him with us for a while.

"Are your wounds healed?"

We felt of our various scrapes and bruises.

John spoke up. "I had the best of it, I suppose. It was frightening for a moment when they buried me, and I couldn't breathe, but …"

"What did you do?" said Julia. "What a helpless feeling!"

"After a moment, I realized that I didn't need to! We're not dependent on those things for life, anymore. We have …" He looked at Jesus, smiling. "We have Life itself!"

"So you just … relaxed?" persisted Julia.

"Yes, I suppose so. Or slept. Something!"

He looked at Jesus. "I think the creatures wanted to know if we could die again, and I was the test. So I decided to be as still as I could for a while, and let them think what they would! Eventually they went away, and I waited for … "

He looked around at us. "Well, for you, I guess!"

"Any remnant of fear left in your heart, from that?" Jesus asked, gently.

John closed his eyes for a moment. "No. I think I'm fine."

"How about you, Julia?" I asked. "I expect he was not too careful with you, when he hauled you to the cave from … wherever you were."

"I'm fine now," she said, checking her hands and knees. "Healed up well, thanks to Linus!" I looked at him, but he just ducked his head, and seemed to smile at Jesus as he did it.

"How can we serve you today?" asked Job, turning to Jesus.

The King smiled. "I have a gift for you." From a bag I had not noticed, he brought out bread that must have been baked an hour earlier, no more, still warm and soft. We eagerly took the rolls he offered.

"These came from Jolina!" exclaimed Job.

Jesus nodded. "And so did this."

He lifted a tall flat-bottomed bowl from the bag, took off its lid, poured a steaming frothy soup into cups, and offered one to each of us. "And I have a few more things for you in here," he said, setting the bag aside, "since everything in there" — he motioned to the cave — "is gone." He leaned back against the rocks.

"John," he said, "is it a concern to you, that you never walked on Earth? That you do not share many of the experiences of the others?"

"No," came the reply, after a moment and a smile. He looked at Jesus. "There are times when I do not understand what they say, but I can always ask."

Jesus nodded.

"And there are times when I understand more than they do, I think."

Jesus laughed. "Good. I too was brutally killed, cut down without cause, but it was a choice I made; yours was not a choice."

John looked down. "But I was spared many a heartache, after the pain of that death, by coming to you that soon," he said, looking up.

"Yes, and I was glad to receive you to myself. What you missed does not matter in Eternity."

He looked at Julia.

"You have done well to ignore the accusations Gadol has made. He did not draw you into self-hatred, or suspicion towards your brothers."

Those Irish eyes twinkled. "He wasn't very creative."

"What did he say, Julia?" asked Job, and she related the taunts Gadol had offered.

Linus said, looking at me, "He told me that you held me in contempt, because of all I did not know, all that had been learned in the thousands of years between us."

I stared. "What did you say?"

"I told him that if that were true, I should hold him in contempt, because of all I knew, all I learned while he slept in his prison cell for just as long!"

"It was well spoken," said Jesus. Looking around at us, he concluded, "None of you have been damaged by the evil one's use of these creatures. Be aware: it will continue."

"Why are they here," asked John, "and how … what should be our bearing towards them?"

Jesus nodded at the question. "They consider themselves the Dominant; they lust for the dominion you possess. They covet the eternal life you possess, and they have lost. Most of all, they seek a way out of their imprisoned state, and hate those who have come from Father. Do what you see Father doing, and His will shall come to pass."

"Jesus," I ventured, "it is not your way to coerce your creation…"

He nodded.

"But when Job healed the beast, he forced it to come to him."

"The Father deals with those made in His image differently than the rest of Creation. Your choices, your will, your freedom are sacred to Him, and He honors whatever choices you make."

He smiled, as He looked around at us.

"Of course, there are consequences to all choices."

Yes, we knew.

"For them, and for the rest of Creation, He deals differently with those in rebellion than those in submission."

And He said no more on the subject.

When we had finished, and simply sat enjoying His presence, He said, "I actually have another gift for you as well."

I could hardly wait for Him to go on, and He knew it as He looked at me. That incredible smile played across His face, that smile that sang of the joy of the Father.

"I promised you a home."

No one said anything. What did he mean? The promise about "go to prepare a place for you" had surely been fulfilled already, with our homes in Heaven.

"Remember that lake you swam in, Julia?"

"Yes," she said, taken aback for a moment.

"You splashed about in it a bit, too, didn't you?" He said, looking at me.

"Now that you mention it, yes!"

"Julia, suppose there were a room looking out over it, facing those mountains to the west? A room about … oh, as high up as as we are from the surf down there?"

"That would be … incredible!"

He looked around at the group. "It's waiting for you!"

"With real chairs!" He added, motioning at the rocks we sat on! Everyone laughed.

"How do we get there?" asked Job.

"I think Julia can show you, and perhaps introduce you to some of her new friends along the way. And don't worry about Leviathan's kin … I'll distract them. It will take them a while to find you, and they won't like it much when they do!"

With that, He was gone. And the soup bowl was full again!

With dusk fading into night, we decided to travel hidden by the darkness. The night air was pleasant and the long blades of grass whispered to each other in the soft breeze as we headed east to the mountains now so familiar. What a change had come, since the rocks and sand and desert heat that greeted our arrival! About midnight we crossed the stream, taking a few minutes to splash in the cool water and fill canteens. The valley and the foothills were alive with creatures large and small; we heard them rustling past our feet, swishing through the air above us, and calling out to each other in the moonlight.

Walking was not tiresome, and the dawn found us approaching the foothills, looking for the pass Julia had first discovered. We turned south, as she had done, and soon found the gap between the low peaks that led across the first ridge. We turned up the ravine, crossed the gap, and worked our way down through the pine and elm, or something very similar to those.

"Something peculiar happened, last time I was here," said Julia, as we looked out over the valley and the lake. "A buck, a doe, and two fawns were here. We spent some time together…"

"You had a little extra time?" I teased.

"No, but I rescheduled some pressing appointments!" she retorted. "We took a nap together, and when I was ready to move on…"

"They made reservations for you at the next stop?"

My joke was lost on her. Apparently reservations were not common at the inns of Ireland, at least in the 6th century!

"When I was ready to move on…" she repeated, cocking an eyebrow at me, "they offered to come help if needed. The buck did, at least."

"How did he make that offer?" asked John.

"Just … just a thought in my mind, really. But I could tell it wasn't from me, and he was looking at me, and … it just seemed obviously from him."

"Did you accept the offer?" Job seemed to take it in stride.

"Yes, actually, I did."

"Good. If you see him, introduce us! Perhaps that's who Jesus meant."

Suddenly I realized the stone outcropping across the lake was not a stone outcropping. There was no cliff there, no stone surface behind it. A mansion rose before us, red roof and gleaming white walls sheltered among low oak and spruce, just beyond the smooth grassy apron surrounding the lake.

"Look at that," I shouted. "It's beautiful!"

Julia stepped up beside me. "Think there are any catfish in that lake?"

"Let's find out!" I laughed, and began skipping and jumping down the slope toward the lake.

When it was all over, Julia was the first in the door. I think getting Linus to tackle me was not entirely fair, but there it is. She won.

The stairs up the front entrance must have been 50 feet wide and 20 steps high. The six stories up to the red tile roof made it just the right height to be majestic in that setting, but without overwhelming the view. Flowers blossomed on porches, balconies, side gardens, walk-ways, everywhere -- brilliant golds and oranges and whites, with soft blue and pale pink scattered among them.

The entry was carpeted with a fabric as soft as the lawn outside, and the walls seemed to have patterns or images that were never quite the same from day to day … or even since the last time you glanced at them. They brought to mind the glories of the creation, sometimes evoking memory of something tiny and other times simulating a grand landscape or panorama of the heavens, but never quite clear enough that you saw it as a picture. Never quite that specific.

The rooms were as big as entire homes where I grew up, with couches and chairs and tables and beds apparently tailored to our taste and preference. When you walked into one, you knew immediately whose room it was, there was no doubt.

That evening we sat on the shore of the lake, watching the glorious sunset over the western ridge. I fashioned a line with a bit of melon fastened to the end, and tossed it out over the water. It dropped to the surface, and floated there serenely.

"No catfish?" Julia was persistent.

I thought about it.

"Bottom feeders!" I said.

That eyebrow came up again.

"Them. The catfish. Wait a minute!"

I found a pebble I could tie near the bait, so I pulled it in. Or, tried to. As soon as the melon moved, it was gone.

"Not catfish, but something!"

My empty line was easy to retrieve. I tied the pebble a foot from the end, then tied a bit of melon shell to the end of the line. Once again, I tossed it as far out as I could.

"Please, I'm really getting hungry…" Julia whined.

The melon rind hit the water, and the pebble splashed right in beside it. A moment later it was clear that the rind had more float than the pebble had sink. Or, it was really shallow out there.

"Julia, you swam out there, right?"

"Sure did."

"How deep is it?"

"I pulled a beautiful stone up from about there ... maybe twice my height?"

"Thanks. I need a bigger weight."

"Need to eat more?"

"Um, no. I need more weight on the line to pull that melon rind down."

The next cast disappeared into the water, and she began singing, "How long, oh Lord, how long..."

Suddenly the line jerked, and released. I pulled. No resistance. The line came up easily.

"I need a hook..."

"To pull a sheep in?" asked Linus. Julia rewarded him with a wink.

I lay back on the grass. "It's late ... the stars are out ... goodnight, everyone." I closed my eyes, pretending to sleep.

There was a moment of silence, that went on ... and I realized too late what it meant. Just as I became suspicious, a flood of cold lake water splashed over my face.

"Aagh, stop!" I cried, but too late. More followed, until I was soaked, and everyone was falling down laughing.

"Come on," I pleaded. "I bathed! Just last month!"

Linus recovered enough to say, "That's why the animals are staying away from us! Now I understand!" And they all collapsed again.

The silence settled over us again, as we looked at the star field above.

"What did you do, on Earth, to earn your days' wages?" asked Linus, rolling over and looking at me.

"Software," I said. No one knew what that was.

How could I explain it?

"You had machines in Rome, Linus? Things that used wheels, and pulleys?"

"Yes, for carts, and lifting things. Building the aqueducts."

"And Julia, you had things like that, too?"

"Sure. And some tools for making pottery and metal pots, and screw presses for wine, is that what you mean?"

"So imagine tools that can work with information, just like those tools work with wine and pots and bricks. Tools that can put numbers together and show the sum of them, or tools that can draw pictures and maps, and tools that can even learn to figure out problems for you."

John looked at me with a bemused smile. Since he had not lived in that world, he had less background to work with in deciphering my words, than the others did. And I was struggling to make a connection for them. Julia had died before the printing press was invented, and Linus knew nothing more current than whatever the Romans used to build roads and chariots.

"My job was to make those tools, and to … to teach those tools how to do things, how to figure things out."

They shook their heads. This was obviously unfathomable.

"Julia, you were a good cook, weren't you? Didn't you tell me that?"

"Yes," she said, scrunching up her face. "The connection?"

"If you wanted to tell someone how to put together flour and spices and tomatoes and lettuce, and make a wonderful meal, you could do it?"

"Of course. Just a list of things to do, one after the other. If you do it right, the food is good. If you do it like Linus, well..."

Linus came up behind her, wrapped his arms around her, and lifted her high in the air. Turning around three times, he set her down again.

"You were saying?" he said.

"Humph."

"So it's like that, Julia."

"Like what?"

"Like making a list of instructions, and then someone ... or something ... that is not smart enough to make up the list, can follow it, and make the salad, or cake, or whatever, the way you said to."

"And that's what you did? You made up recipes for tools to follow?"

"Exactly."

This was too much for them.

"How did you die?" asked Julia, changing the subject.

I told them about the airplane crash.

"Your family?" asked Julia?

I smiled at her kindness. "Thank you, sweet lady. My wife and two beautiful kids were still at home, one of them just a baby. Jesus showed me their hearts, and the provision he was making for them. I'll see them soon, of course. Can't wait."

But I knew that she knew that feeling for herself. It had been long enough for her that she had already welcomed her own family Home, and many generations of grandchildren besides.

"Julia, tell us about Ireland. Tell us about when you and your family set out to tell the world about Jesus, when the lands east of you had all but forgotten Him."

Twenty-One

It was still dark when Grandfather called me.

"Julia!"

I groaned, and he laughed.

"Time to go save the world, sweet child!"

I groaned again, trying to hold on to what little sleep remained. Sure, it was an adventure, to leave home for … how long? I was afraid to even think about it. To see Bangor, and hear the monks singing the psalms there, and see the Vale of Angels … then across the water to reach Scotland, then walk down into Britain, then across water again to Gaul, following the steps of Columbanus… And I was excited to go. But did we have to leave before the sun even rose?

I pulled the blanket over my head again, and things got quiet. Too quiet.

"Mac!" I did not even have to look, to see who brought the goat in to lick my bare toes! "Get him out of here!"

Father burst out laughing, and the family all joined in.

Mother's flute was softly caressing the 23rd Psalm, and Mac and Cenn were pulling on their cloaks and boots when I made it to the kitchen.

"Is it awake yet, then?" they laughed at me, and I poked them. Both. Brothers are for poking, and mine especially so!

"I can outrun you both, and you know it!"

"And then sleep in our arms, while we carry you across the next ten fields!"

"Is that a promise?" asked Father. Everyone knew who normally ended up carrying me! I jumped on his lap, and tried to find his spoon.

"This is mine … that is yours!" he whispered, setting me on the stool with a bowl of hot oatmeal and a mug of goat's milk waiting, and the flute played on.

By the time I finished breakfast and pulled on my sandals, everyone was ready. My pack seemed light enough, but I knew by dusk it would be too heavy by twice!

"Where to, first?"

"The front gate, if you can make it that far!" teased Cenn, so I was standing there by the time he came out the door. If I can make it that far!

The real answer was, of course, the church, where others were waiting. Twenty or more were going this time, going to walk the Gospel across Britain, into Gaul, and as much further as we could go.

At nineteen I was ready to be married and be starting my own family, and this would likely be the last adventure for me, at least for many years. Most of my friends from playgrounds and classrooms now had babes in their arms, and though I envied their romances and new lives, I was fine with waiting a bit longer.

Mac came up alongside me. A year apart, we were not twins, but could have been, and loved to tease and have our jokes on the others, more than the rest.

"Are you really comfortable with your decision?"

"You mean, not marrying yet?"

"Yes," he replied, "and making a journey that we know so little about."

"Look at them," I said, as we topped the hill before the church. Many of our friends had gathered to see us off. "Look at them, all my friends, everyone I've grown up with, all holding their babes, all with their husbands."

He watched me as we walked.

"Yes, I want to go."

"What if we never come back?"

I stopped and turned him toward me, letting Mother walk past with my baby sister bundled in her arms.

"What if?"

He smiled, and I saw in his eyes the same settled confidence that was in mine.

"What if God has an adventure for us that He offers no one else?" I asked.

"Then we'll take it!" he shouted, and we ran laughing to catch up to the others.

Abran came to meet us, and especially to meet me, I think. I believe he would have proposed already if this trip were not planned, and it was a grief in my heart not to have that gift, if he indeed intended to give it. But that was behind me now, or maybe for later.

Others gathered around, many offering a loaf or some vegetables to be packed in our sacks. Mr. Branson had made us a cart, just as he promised, and the axles looked to have grease enough to get us around the world before they squeaked. He had hitched Sassy to it, and both the cart and the donkey were his gift to the travelers, since he had not strength enough to go with us. Father hugged him, and we all did the same.

Master Sinelli called us together.

"Let us ask God's blessing on those who go, and those who stay," he said. We bowed our heads.

"Our Father, let your grace be over these as they travel, and your words be in their mouths as they tell the world about your mercy and love."

Master Sinelli's wife began a hymn, one they had learned from the monks, and the sun broke over the horizon as we finished.

Soon the farewells were done, and we were starting the long trip. How long would it take? Would we ever come back? No one knew. I could barely say goodby to Mother; I could not imagine how Father could do so, but she and the baby could not travel with us.

That night we camped in a freshly cut barley field near Northampton, where some oaks gave us shelter and a stream ran nearby. The embers drifted up from our small fire, and Father cooked some salt pork and potatoes for us. Stars filled the deep blackness of the cloudless sky, and I lay thinking about what might lay ahead.

I woke stiff and cold. The hard reality of the journey began to sink in. Paul's journeys came to mind and the list of his difficulties took vivid new color in my mind.

Master Natalis seemed to be the leader, along with Father. They sat together over a Bible after breakfast and led some singing before we gathered our things to begin again.

Late that afternoon we came to the sea. Mac helped load everyone's things into the boats that were waiting. Cenn knew boats a little, from rowing around a lake with Master Sinelli's sons; he helped get oars in place and got some instruction about the sails. Each little boat had a single sail, a rudder in the back, and two oars fastened to the side rails.

The inn by the water had room for everyone, after a fashion. We shared a room, and other families did the same. I slept on the floor with Mac and Cenn. Father used the cot, and we insisted he take it when he offered it to me. I wanted none of the teasing that would invite! The big room downstairs had rough tables and benches for a crowd, but few were there that night. We had our fill of roast lamb and stewed carrots with hot bread and butter.

As dawn broke we climbed into those fragile, unsteady little boats. I sat by one of the oars, but Cenn moved me to the front and took that place, smiling as though there were a joke. I missed it, I guess.

Father began whistling the tune Mother used for the Psalm as we pushed off into the rising wind. I wondered if he chose the one about "still waters" on purpose, as the boat slipped around on the waves and tilted so close to the water on one side and then the other. The wind caught our little sail and jerked us forward. The water jumped up at me. I grabbed the sides even tighter.

"Julia."

"Yes, Cenn?"

"You'll break it."

"What?"

"The boat!"

Everyone behind me laughed, and I looked at my hands, white from gripping the wooden rails. I took a breath, and tried to relax; perhaps I did, by the time we landed hours later.

But then I couldn't walk: the ground was moving just as the water had!

We could not afford to stay at the inns, traveling across the countryside with no way of earning our keep. And no one would house and feed a group of twenty travelers. It was time to separate into much smaller groups. We needed to find shelter and food from the people we went to help.

I was surprised. I thought we would all travel together, a miniature church making our way across the land, telling about Jesus. Suddenly I felt much more risk than before.

Father elected to keep our family together, so we four set out on our own. We traveled about six hours each day, then sought out a small church or the leaders of a small town and asked for lodging. We sang for them, talked about a Scripture or two, and prayed for them when we could. Some welcomed us, and some were quite skeptical, not being believers themselves. Most had heard the name Jesus, but I was amazed at how many knew Him not.

Some in our church had received "the filling," as they called it, and seemed to sense His presence more than others and be especially confident in prayer. Cenn was one of those. At 24 he had always been the brother I most adored, and seemed most intent on really knowing God, not just knowing about Him.

When we came to Harrelton the family that welcomed us to stay with them seemed sad. They hardly spoke at all. We soon learned that the mother was quite ill, expected to die. The father prepared a simple meal, and they left us to ourselves to make do in the gathering room. A low fire kept the chill away. We bedded down.

"Julia."

Cenn was crouched next to me as he woke me with a touch on my cheek.

"What can it be, Cenn? Is ought wrong?"

He frowned and seemed uncertain. "I want to pray for her."

I glanced to the back of the house. The light of a candle glowed under the wooden door. No sound came from there.

I looked back to Cenn. "Has God spoken to you?"

He shook his head. "Nothing like that, really. But I can't sleep, and it seems the thought will not let me be."

He looked sharply at me. "Do you think it might be the Spirit Himself, urging me on?"

I had no experience of that myself, and neither did he, to my knowledge. But there was a certainty in his eyes that set my heart pounding.

"Let's ask Father."

We woke him, and Father listened without speaking. After a bit, he roused himself, and in one of those moments that made me love him even more, simply said, "If it be God, we surely don't want to miss it!"

He pulled on a cloak, walked quietly to the door into the sleeping room, listened for a moment, and returned.

"There's tears falling in there. I'm going to knock. Are you ready?"

Cenn nodded, glancing nervously at me. I grabbed his arm and took my place at his side, not wanting to be left out.

Father returned to the door and knocked softly.

The door opened slightly and he whispered back and forth with the father we had met earlier. The man then came out and closed the door carefully. He came to Cenn and looked intently into his face.

"She burns with fever, son."

Cenn nodded.

"I cannot believe she'll live 'til morning. I've seen this before."

Cenn looked down. The pain in the man's face and the weariness in his eyes startled me. Cenn apparently became even more sure, and looked back at the hopelessness staring out from those tearful eyes.

"I can't say, sir, of course. But God be good, and His love is real. If you'd allow us, we'd like to gather around her and ask His touch."

After a moment the man dropped his gaze. He swallowed hard and nodded. Leading the way back to the bedroom, he spoke briefly to his wife then opened the door wide for us to enter.

She lay face up, a cloth across her brow. Her young son waved a fan over her with a weariness that bespoke hours of the same.

Cenn approached the head of the bed. She turned to look at him. Her face burned, showing the heat of the fever even in this bit of candle light.

I dropped to the side of the bed and took her hand. Hot and sweaty, it had no strength left in it that I could tell. Her eyes closed, then slowly opened again.

Father and Mac joined her husband on the other side of the bed, and he pushed aside the cast-off sheets and blankets piled there so they could draw near.

We stood and knelt in silence for some time. Cenn bowed his head, apparently waiting for the leading he sought from God. Finally he looked up and simply said, "Father, we bring your daughter before you. She needs your touch, and we know your love."

Then he looked at her, put his hand on top of mine where I held her, and said, "In the name of Jesus, receive healing. Be well."

We waited; I certainly had no idea what else to do. She closed her eyes. Her shallow breathing continued as before.

Father nudged us and Mac, and they moved to the door. Cenn helped me up, and we followed them, with a nod to the husband. He simply watched us go. Had we brought a flicker of hope to his desperate soul with no reason to have done so?

We settled back into our blankets without speaking. Father hugged Cenn before going to his place.

Morning came suddenly, though I thought the pain I had seen in the man's eyes would haunt me through the night. We quickly gathered our things and prepared to slip out without disturbing the family again.

The door to the bedroom opened, and the woman stood there. Her hair was combed. Her dress was fresh. Her husband stood behind her with tears running down onto his beard. The little boy stood at her side, hugging her as though he never intended to let go again. She came to Cenn without speaking, wrapped her arms around him, and wept on his shoulder. Tears flowed down my face as well. Finally she stepped back to her husband's side.

"As soon as the door closed behind you, I felt the fever break," she said quietly. The hand of Almighty God is with you. Where do you travel, what do you do?"

It took Father a minute to clear his throat, and be able to speak. His hand kept going to his eyes.

"We go to tell Britain, and Gaul, and anyone who will listen, that God is real. That He loves, and we are his beloved," answered Father. He returned her gaze for another long moment, and smiled, and wiped his eyes again. "Not by ourselves, certainly. There are several families with us, and we'll join with the monks leaving from Bangor when we reach the coast."

"How will you live, on the road?"

"We'll work for our keep, and ask shelter and food from those we can help," said Father, looking around at us to see what we might add. "I can cook a bit," I offered, and Mac is good with an axe! Cenn knows animals, and has a gentle touch with them."

"And with people, I would say!" she laughed.

"Must you be going now?" asked the husband. "Are you trying to reach somewhere before the winter sets in?"

"Is there aught we could do for you, friend?" asked Father. "We have enough time, I think, to meet the others, if we stay a bit."

"There are some here who would be glad to hear what you have to say," the husband offered, "and with no grown children to help me, there's a bit of repair I could use an extra hand with! My name's Benedict, and this is Ida. My son is Brendan. My apologies, you've spent the night in our home and we've not even introduced ourselves. Our grief, you know, we were about to lose her."

We introduced ourselves, and settled our things back against the wall in the big room.

"Let me be gone a bit, and we'll have a gathering this eve. Ida?" He looked at his wife, and she turned to the kitchen. Wonderful smells were soon filling the air.

We sat to breakfast with a will. She served us hot oatmeal with goat's milk and fresh melons, insisting we pray for them before we ate, and to help her offer God her thanks. Brendan just watched us, and said not a word all morning.

In the afternoon we lay down for a bit to rest. Brendan sat near Cenn.

"Do you know God, then?" he asked.

Cenn sat up and leaned his back against the timbers of the wall.

"How old are you, Brendan?"

"I'll be eight in a month."

"Can you write?"

"Some of my letters. And I can read a bit! Mother's a good teacher."

"I'm sure she is. Have you read anything of the Scripture at all?"

"In what?"

"The Bible," said Cenn.

"Don't rightly know what that is, sir."

"Never mind, then. It's letters and histories written by the people of God, for hundreds of years. But you asked about knowing God?"

"Yes. Tell me about that!"

I sat up, and snuggled up against my brother. "Yes, please," I added, looking up at him with my most sincere smile. He winked at me.

"He's your father, for ever and ever, just like your pa is your father here on earth."

"I have two fathers?"

I laughed.

"When we accept God's love for us, we become part of his family. He becomes our Father, not just the one who created us."

"How do you know all that?"

"People who know him tell other people, and we all get to decide if we want to be in the family. Do you?"

"Can you see him?"

Cenn frowned.

"Sure," I said. "You already have!"

Brendan stared at me. "When? What does he look like?"

"Last night, he looked a lot like Cenn!"

Brendan turned to Cenn, scrunching his eyes up and staring at him closely.

Finally he turned back to me. "I don't understand."

Cenn laughed. "None of us do, really. It's a mystery. But when Jesus was healing people, and teaching them, he said if you've seen him, you've seen the Father. What do you think he meant?"

Brendan lay down on the mat and stared at the ceiling.

I said, "Brendan, how did your mother get well?"

He sat up, very serious. "You didn't do that, did you?"

"No," said Cenn, equally serious. "I have no power. God did that. Your father in heaven did that. He lives in us, somehow, and lets us work with Him as he loves people. As he heals people. As he tells people about himself."

"That's what you're doing now!"

"Yes, Brendan," laughed Cenn, "that's exactly what we're doing now!"

"So, Brendan," said Mac, who had been listening to all this, "do you want …"

The door opened, and Benedict came in, rubbing his hands. "Gettin' colder. You folks comfortable?"

"Indeed we are," said Father, sitting up. "Have you arranged a meeting?"

"Believe I have, believe I have. About twenty or so will join us this evening, just a bit after dinnertime."

Twenty-Two

The next morning we began drawing maps, spreading a roll of paper, or parchment, I'm not sure what it was, on the huge table in the dining area. Julia had made some notes of this part of the world from her earlier walks, and I had seen more from Gadol's back.

I also had a good sense of the coastline going north from our original cave, and John described the southern coast for us. Job had explored the mountains north of this ridge, so we added that as well.

"How big is this planet?"

"Twice Earth, I think," said Job.

"With ice at the poles?"

The others did not understand the question.

"Earth," I explained, has "ice caps," areas that are always frozen and covered with snow and ice, at both ends."

"How can a ball have 'ends'…?" asked John.

"Think of a spinning ball. The suns and moons rise in the sky, go over us, then drop down the other side, because we are spinning towards them, then away from them."

He nodded.

"The parts that face the sun, the middle of the ball, get more heat, and have night and day, as they pass under the sun. The parts that always face sideways to the sun, don't get as much heat from the sun … it never shines directly on them … so they're colder. They freeze."

"So," he asked, turning to Job, "will this planet have ice on the … on the ends?" He smiled at me, as he said that.

"Sounds right to me."

"How far would it be from here?"

Job and I looked at each other. He had been a commander of men, a builder, a great man in his time, so I think the discipline of thinking through a hard question came naturally to him.

"If I'm right, that we are twice the size of Earth… how long, to travel from the waist of the planet, to the … to the top … do you think?"

I laughed. "By horse? By foot? By airplane?" They frowned at the last.

"Didn't you say that the last time you were on one of those, it crashed?" asked Julia.

What could I say? She had me.

"On the back of Gadol, I think it would take a full day, maybe two, to reach areas with snow, and twice that to reach the caps."

"Without stopping," I added. "Assuming we're at the equator. The waist," I added, as John looked at me.

"How long to go sideways?" asked Linus.

"You mean to go the direction the planet turns … toward or away from the sunrise … and go all the way around?"

I remembered the story about the man circling the earth in 80 days.

"So, Job, do you think it's twice the diameter, the thickness, of Earth, or twice the circumference?"

"I suppose I was thinking diameter…" he replied. "That makes a difference, doesn't it!"

"The reason I ask," I said, "is that a story is told on Earth about a man who wagered he could travel around the earth in 80 days. This was in a time when they had steam-driven engines, so he could travel faster than a horse could run for large portions of the voyage."

"But there were times of delay, perhaps?"

"Of course."

"So if we walk instead of ride, and it's twice as far around, and we have more delays -- for lack of boats, and inns, and such -- that's perhaps a year."

"Or more."

"Are there horses here?" asked Julia.

"I should have guessed you would ride!" I said. "But … in Ireland, in that time? There were horses?"

"No," she retorted, "but did you notice what He rode when He sent us off?"

"Here!" I exclaimed. "I mean … There … at Home!"

She curtsied. "At your service, should you ever need a ride!"

"Well!" I turned to Job. "Are there horses here?"

"Haven't seen any," he said.

"Yet."

We lay on the lawn under the brilliant sky. The second moon had just dropped beneath the tree line, and the deep black of the sky set off the millions of stars like diamonds on velvet.

"There's the Throne," said Julia. "Look, low over the trees behind us."

"And my favorite, the Turtle," said John. "What a perfect likeness… if you don't mind the stubby tail being missing!"

"And Leviathan," laughed Julia. "You should have seen Gadol's expression when I told him we had named a constellation for his father!"

"Job, what do you suppose is their intent?" I asked.

"I think they're ready to be done with us," he replied. "They don't care about the planet, they'd rather be somewhere else anyway. But if they've got to be here, they'd rather have it to themselves."

"And they hate Father," said John. "That's what drives them."

"Yes," agreed Job. "Hatred of the One who put them here, who waits so patiently for their repentance and allegiance."

"I think His patience makes them as crazy as anything else," said Linus. "They don't understand it. Maybe they …"

"… hate themselves, so they can't abide someone willing to love them or forgive them?"

"Maybe, Julia, but that's more the way people think," I answered. "With them, I think it's simpler … rebellion, hatred of God's authority over them, the pride of … Self."

We were quiet for a while, bathing in the glory of the lights above us.

"O Lord my God, when I in awesome wonder …" I began the old hymn quietly, "… consider all the worlds thy hands have made; I see the stars, I hear the rolling thunder, thy power throughout the universe displayed…" I left off, feeling quite unable to properly praise the glory above us.

"That's beautiful," said Julia. "Is there more? That did not sound like the end!"

"Oh. Yes. Can anyone help me?"

"I learned it not long ago," said Job. "I'll sing with you. You'll not be able to guess who taught me!"

"Well, then," I laughed, "let's teach it to our friends!" And we began with the chorus.

"Then sings my soul, my Savior God, to thee,
    how great thou art! How great thou art!
Then sings my soul, my Savior God, to thee,
    how great thou art! How great thou art!"

"Which verse is next?" asked Job, when we both paused. "I don't recall."

"And when I think that God, His son not sparing,
    sent him to die, I scarce can take it in…
that on the cross, my burden gladly bearing,
    he bled and died to take away my sin."

The others listened quietly. We sang the chorus again, then the last verse -- or at least the only other verse we could remember.

"When Christ shall come, with shout of acclamation,
    and take me home, what joy shall fill my heart!
Then I shall bow in humble adoration, and there proclaim,
    'My God, how great thou art!'"

And with one more time through the chorus, we fell silent again.

"That's all very well," said Linus, "but you didn't!"

"Didn't what?" I replied, after thinking about it for a moment.

"You didn't bow! I was there! There was no bow … and I don't remember your saying anything like 'how great thou art', either, at the time!"

He was right. Stunned amazement I remembered, but I certainly had not quoted a 19th century song to Jesus when I met him!

"What could anyone say," asked Linus, "but 'thank you'? I could only look at Him and cry, and laugh, and cry … it was so good."

We lay quiet for a long time. Shooting stars flew over occasionally.

"You know how we can see so much better?" asked Linus.

"Sure. Amazing."

"Has anyone explored other senses? Smell, hearing, even taste?"

"Pretty much the same, for me," said John. "Hadn't noticed any difference."

Julia rolled over and punched him.

"What?" John exclaimed, laughing. "What did I say?"

"I've noticed it with hearing," I said. "Out in the forest, I sat and listened for the smallest sounds I could hear. Some deer were feeding on the other side of the valley, so far away I barely noticed them. I began listening, and tried to focus in on just them … there was so much going on that was closer! But finally I'm sure I was listening to one of the fawns chewing on the grass. And when the buck was startled by something, and snorted …oh, my! I jumped! It was half an hour before I could really relax again!"

"Me, too," agreed Julia. "Especially in the forest. Little animals underground, things moving through the grass at night… even fish in the lake, I think!"

"What were they discussing?" asked John.

"Who?"

"The fish. In the lake. Just curious."

She rolled over and punched him again.

"What?"

We all laughed, and settled into the quiet night again. The number of stars and galaxies easily visible was astounding.

"Job, is Father sending others out, to the other stars?"

What a thought. On planets all over that amazing sky, to planets scattered across more light-years than once-born man had been able to comprehend, others would be going out to call worlds into fruition.

"Soon," he whispered. "Soon."

"When will Gadol and the others find us?"
"Soon," he whispered again. "Very soon."

Twenty-Three

It was an hour after lunch when Job called us together in the great room downstairs.

"Gadol is circling above. The others seem to be on the ground, perhaps coming in quietly while we watch Gadol."

We looked out the windows where he pointed. Gadol was making no effort to hide himself.

"What will we do, when they come?" I asked.

"It's His battle, not ours. Let's ask."

We gathered close.

"They are coming to get us, Father," murmured Job. "Show us what to do. We wait on your direction, your guidance. Like your son Hezekiah, we want to do it Your way, not ours."

John spoke up, after a few moments. "I think … I'm not sure, but I think He wants us to welcome them."

We all looked at him. Welcoming these beasts was the last thing I wanted to do.

"I think that's right, John," said Job. "I think His goal is their redemption, and He's offering them every last opportunity."

"What if they don't take it?" asked Julia. "What happens if they're not interested?"

Job smiled. "I expect we'll find out." He pointed out the window, where Gadol had landed on the lawn in front of the house. "Let's go say hello!"

We walked out on the porch and spread out across the steps. Gadol stood a hundred yards away, not moving. The larger sun was directly overhead, the sky was deep blue, the day was beautiful and calm. Job rubbed his face and looked up at the cloudless sky.

A rustle in the forest to our right told us where another of them had approached.

"Tontal, I would guess," laughed Job. He's the biggest, and would have the hardest time being quiet!"

"So the other two will come from behind the house," Julia said, turning around to glance through the doors.

"Let's invite some guests to the party," said Job. "What do you think?"

I understood immediately. "Wonderful idea. I'll go send out the invitation." I ran into the house, grabbed the railing and flew upstairs. We used the top floor as an observatory, and my digiroo was there. I unlatched the big window facing north and set the horn on the windowsill.

With a deep breath, I started a long, low wail, and slowly brought it up to the highest pitch I could form. When I ran out of breath I pulled it away, rested for a few seconds, then blew it again. When that was done and I recovered some wind, I did it once more with all the breath I could muster, a long, brooding, penetrating call across the forest and the valley.

There was nothing else to be done. I ran back downstairs. Gadol was still out front, motionless, and Tontal had emerged from the woods on the right. A huge black thing, with dark green mottling his sides and belly, I could believe he was the bully of the crowd.

A crashing sound broke the silence to our left and a third beast came into view. Light grey with yellow on his chest, he was smaller than Tontal but the look in his eye was the same.

They began walking forward.

"Only three?" I asked quietly.

"Oh, yes, didn't I tell you?" replied Job, and he raised his voice to address Gadol.

"Gadol!"

A low growl was the answer.

"Aren't you going to introduce us to your friends?"

Gadol began to speak, and Tontal interrupted him.

"Shut up."

Job turned to face Tontal. I stepped up to his right side, and the others moved to his left, between him and Gadol.

"Livya-Tontal, of the planet 'Nsela at Mintaka, son of Leviathan, ward of 'Athelkan: Welcome to our home."

"Your home," growled Tontal, "your home indeed. Your grave!"

"Have you not heard, Tontal?" said Linus.

"What?"

"'Appointed once to die' ..."

"And we've all done that already!" grinned Julia. "You're too late!"

"If you are in pieces, you cannot live!" roared Tontal, and he stepped forward.

"Like Ruunt?" asked Job.

Tontal froze. Turning to Gadol, he demanded, "How did he know?"

Gadol appeared equally surprised.

"It doesn't matter!" spat Guntel, speaking for the first time.

Tontal looked at Guntel, and the smaller animal froze.

"You ... shut ... up ... too."

Job turned to me. "Are our friends on the way?"

"I expect them any minute."

"Tell me about Ruunt," said Job, turning again to Tontal.

"He is none of your concern."

"You have committed murder, Tontal. The only one that has happened on this world. His blood cries out from the ground. It is my concern. Your life is in my hands. I have dominion here."

"Dominion," he repeated slowly.

Gadol backed up a few steps, and sat down. Guntel started forward, shook his head, and looked at Gadol. Gadol slowly swung his head sideways. Guntel stopped, then slowly backed up to the edge of the woods.

Tontal stared at Job, then bellowed, standing to his full height. "You? Dominion over me, a Son of Leviathan? Dominion over the Dominant?"

Job said nothing.

"I am of 'Nsela now, anyway, not your filthy world."

"Then you should not have come here. Now you are mine. Does 'Athelkan know where you are?"

Tontal roared again, and threw himself towards us. Job stood without moving, whispering to us, "It's not our battle. Don't move."

The beast landed an arm's length from us, towering over us with his rough belly heaving in our faces, his hot breath smoldering over us, his stench overwhelming us. His great claw was high above us, and as he landed, it swept down to strike us all in one blow.

And stopped.

Silence covered the valley, and the day was suddenly much brighter.

From behind Tontal came the silver voice of 'Athelkan. "Tontal, what are you doing?"

A choking, rasping sound squeezed from his throat, with no visible movement in his body. Job motioned us to step back, and we eased away from the living statue. Out from under his looming body, Job turned towards Gadol, and strolled down the steps toward him. I gawked at Tontal, then pulled myself away to follow Job.

Gadol was staring at Tontal as we walked up to him. As we came before him, I turned, following his eyes, and saw Tontal in the same position, unmoving. His wings, however, were shriveling as we watched, drying up and shrinking. I could not pull my eyes away. In a few moments they were gone, leaving just a lump of bone on his shoulders where they had been.

"Gadol."

Job's voice was soft. I looked back. Gadol's eyes snapped to Job's face, and there was a fear in them I had not seen before.

"Do you desire the same fate?"

He looked back at Tontal, then glanced at Job, then stared again at Tontal.

"Gadol."

He wrenched his eyes away from his kin, and looked at Job, a terrified expression now contorting his face.

Job's voice was almost kind. "Go, Gadol, find a place to live on this planet where you can be at peace, and do not torment a living thing."

Gadol slowly nodded.

"Perhaps the door is still open for you to turn, to accept the One for who He is. Ruunt is gone. Tontal will never fly again, and may wither away in his hatred and bitterness. What will be your fate?"

Gadol did not answer. Everything about him begged permission to leave, and he stood rooted in place, held by Job's gaze.

Finally, Job said, "You may go." Gadol turned and leapt into the sky, not looking back, and was out of sight within moments.

"It's a rich, full planet now," I said. "There will be plenty of places for him to live, far from people and most creatures."

"And being physical, he may just age and die here," suggested John.

"Shall we greet our third guest?" suggested Julia.

We walked back up the lawn. Tontal was on his belly with 'Athelkan before him, and their conversation was not something we could hear. As we approached, 'Athelkan turned to Job.

"My friend, you have been ill-treated by my ward. I will return him to 'Nsela, and without wings, I cannot imagine he will find a way to return. This should be the last you see of him."

"Thank you, 'Athelkan. Let us speak at length, when you can return."

"As you say."

He turned back to Tontal and waved a hand over the prostrate creature. A wrapping of light, a thick and palpable luminescent blanket, became visible encasing Tontal. It grew brighter, and 'Athelkan likewise shone brighter and brighter.

"Farewell, children of Adam," he intoned, including us all with a smile and a sweep of his hand. "All of creation has groaned in travail, waiting for you to be revealed."

And they were gone. The dimmer light of the massive sun overhead gradually became normal again.

Linus turned to Guntel, and discovered he was gone. "Where did the other one go?" We looked around. He had apparently slipped away.

Suddenly we realized we were not alone, by any means. Deer, bear, a dozen horses, hundreds of smaller creatures and a few much bigger ones, surrounded the clearing and spread down the lawn to the lake.

"Welcome, friends!"

They chirped and hooted and snorted and yowled, and there was no doubt they understood the welcome.

A gruff bellowing and snorting came from somewhere behind the house. We looked to the northern corner of the huge building and Guntel came backing up, one slow step at a time, as a bull rhinoceros pushed him nose to nose. A great eagle perched on his shoulders and every time

Guntel made any motion to lift a wing, the eagle stabbed the top of his head and Guntel howled.

Linus began laughing at the sight, and before they got halfway across the lawn to where we stood we were all helpless in tears.

The parade stopped and Guntel glanced around. Seeing Job, he sat down suddenly, pulling himself into a subservient lump before the man with Dominion.

"What shall we do?" asked Job, looking around at us. Linus stepped up to Guntel, and waited. Guntel slowly pulled his eyes off Job, and looked at the man standing before him.

"Tontal has been a bully. So has Gadol."

Guntel slowly nodded.

"Tontal has lost the ability to fly, and will soon be dead of bitterness and hatred. Leviathan is held on Earth, and will not leave. The rebellion in his heart will kill him. Gadol will hide for years, and probably die in his hatred and fear."

Guntel stared, and had no response.

"You are now free of them. What will you do?"

"I left 'Nra," replied Guntel slowly. "The One will be displeased. Will I be crippled, too?"

"What will you do?" repeated Linus. "You are free to choose, as God's creatures always have been. But it is time for you to choose. Your brothers cannot choose for you."

Guntel dropped his head, and scuffed his snout in the dirt and grass. He looked up at Linus, then rubbed his nose in the ground a bit more.

"My world is a wasteland," he said, glancing around at the rich forest, the deep grass, the sweet blue water, and a hint of rainclouds off to the west. "A hot, dry wasteland."

He looked at us. "And there's no one there. It is empty."

"What will you do?" insisted Linus. "If you reject the One, you reject us, and the wastelands are the best you will have."

Guntel stared at the ground, then looked over where Tontal had been stripped. He stared at the ground again.

Around us the creatures who had gathered were completely silent. They seemed to understand what was happening.

"I will speak with the One."

Guntel stood and walked slowly through the silent crowd to the edge of the lake, eyes on the ground. He then stood absolutely still, head raised, looking out over the lake, over the mountain ridges beyond, looking to a place far beyond physical sight. An hour passed, and no one moved. We looked at each other and waited.

Finally Guntel bowed his head.

"Look!" exclaimed Julia, and we all turned our attention back to the figure standing by the lake. He seemed to be growing. The coarse gray skin with blotches of greenish yellow was now shimmering, silken smooth, and rippling with color as though he had slipped into a robe knit of precious jewels. His grotesque, knobby wings stretched out into long, powerful things. Deep velvet burgundy at the shoulders trailed to royal purple at the tips. Muscle rippled across his back and shoulders. He rose to stand on hind feet, and we stepped back involuntarily at how tall he now stood. He slowly turned and walked carefully through the crowd, looking about with ruby eyes and an expression in his face that we had not seen on these creatures before. When he reached Job he stood for a moment without speaking. His newfound beauty was stunning.

"I have decided. I have spoken with Him, and He has accepted me. Is there a place for me here?"

"Woohoo," shouted Julia. Turning to the watching animals, she cried out, "He's decided! He's one of us!" Their cacophony erupted again.

Twenty-Four

Three weeks later, Job suggested we take a trip.

"What do you have in mind?" asked John.

"We have Orion to tend, not just 'Nsol."

"You mean … you mean all the planets, of all the stars, in the constellation?" I was struggling to get my mind around his suggestion. He smiled and waited.

"How many is that?" asked Julia.

"I think we'll know when we're done!" laughed Linus.

"Well, where did you have in mind?"

"For now, just around this planet, but next …"

"We really haven't seen much of this one, actually," said John.

"Right. So I've been busy. Let me show you something!" Job led us back through the house to a large room at the bottom of the first floor that had become a workroom. He had built a loom, I suppose, though I had never really seen one, and had great sheets of cloth spread over the floor.

"What is it?"

"Maybe if I show you this, at least one person can guess!" We followed him out the back door to find a large basket formed of branches and woven vines, large enough for all of us and more to stand in. I began to have an idea.

"I'm guessing the only thing you need now is hot air, and Guntel can provide plenty of that!" I suggested.

"You, my friend, have guessed my secret. I was paying attention to your story, wasn't I! Tell the others!"

"You remember my story about a man going around Earth?"

They did.

"Job quizzed me later about that, and I told him how they used a 'hot air balloon' to travel -- a basket that floated in the air, held up by a bag of hot air above them. The air rises, when it is warmer than the air around it, and will carry things … will carry us! … up in the air! Right?"

Job nodded.

"And since Guntel can fly along with us, and reheat the air when needed, I'm guessing Job is ready to travel!"

And he was.

"But where did the cloth come from?"

"Surely you remember something of my story," he replied. "If I know anything, I know what to do with sheep, and there are herds all over this land!"

We had ropes woven within a few days, and since Job also understood orchards, we had plenty of food to load into the basket for the trip. A nice addition to the normal rigging was a harness for Guntel so he could pull us in whatever direction looked interesting. We would not be at the mercy of the winds for steering.

As the morning broke, we climbed into the basket for a test run. Guntel had filled the balloon and it strained at its mooring ropes. No one wanted to stay behind, so the basket was full. Fall was coming, and the brisk air freshened us all. As we rose above the pasture and lake, drifting eastward towards the peaks we had never crossed, the air cooled even more.

"Guntel, let's go south of that peak, or this will be a very short trip!" called Job. Guntel flew under us, poked his neck through the harness loop, and turned south. We jerked hard as he reached the length of the rope, and he glanced back.

"We're fine," I shouted. "Maybe a little slower next time!" I have to believe he grinned.

The ridge was high, sharp, and barren where we drifted over it into the rising sun. The backlit forest stretched before us as far as we could see. To the south, large birds flew westward, bright white in the clear blue sky.

"We're coming into Fall, Job," commented John. "We could head south, if it gets too cold, and pick our season! Isn't that the way it would work?"

Job looked at me. He had not traveled more than a hundred miles from home, in his life.

"That's exactly right, John. I think we're north of the equator, the center line, so moving south would warm us up. On the other hand, since you've never seen snow …"

"I have, and we're not dressed for it!" declared Julia.

A broad river emerged, flowing from somewhere north of us down from the mountain range, dividing the forest in a long, lazy line. The ground sloped down, and great plains drifted towards us. Guntel had slipped out of the harness and gone down among the treetops, so the soft breeze carried us gently west and a little south.

The plains were high in some sort of grass and herds of animals roamed in them.

"Those are huge!" exclaimed Linus. "We are way up in the air, and look at them!"

"What do you think?" asked Job. "Water buffalo?"

"Not much water, for water buffalo," I said. "Buffalo, bison, some sort of cattle. Grazing on the grasses, drinking from the river, unlimited room to roam, and no predators. They'll do just fine!"

An eagle drifted down the range from our left, and cruised over to visit.

"Come join us!" called Julia, and it circled the basket, eyeing the great balloon. Finally it floated over and perched on the edge of the basket. It was heavy enough, the basket dropped on that side, and rocked for a while after he landed.

The great bird cocked its head, looked at each of us, and waited.

"Swalea!" cried Julia. "Is it you?"

He bowed towards her, and turned to face out. Leaning forward, he dropped towards the forest, waiting to spread his wings until he seemed about to smash into the trees. As he turned level with the ground, his speed became apparent.

"Wow. He was moving!" I marveled. "You know, some people in my time had learned to make wings that would let them float on the wind …"

They all laughed.

"What?"

"We can just see you doing it!" laughed Linus. "We can see you already!"

That evening we gathered in the great room for dinner and talked of our plans to sail around the world.

"Job," I said, suddenly sitting up. Everyone looked at me.

"What are the cords we came to loose, after all?"

Job laughed, stretching his legs out and folding his hands behind his head.

"I thought at first … well, really I had no idea. Did you?"

We shook our heads.

"After talking with 'Athelkan, I thought it was the light paths between the stars, the paths that many of the spirit beings use to travel the universe."

"But those aren't just in Orion… and what would it mean to 'loose' them?" asked John.

"Exactly. 'Athelkan had no other suggestions, but that didn't seem to fit."

We waited.

"Have we grown any tobacco yet?" said Job, after a few minutes. "I've been thinking of carving a pipe, and trying that out!"

I rubbed my face in my hands. "Job. Please. What were the cords?"

He smiled. He knew he could get a reaction from me anytime he wanted to.

"Did you ever read Paul's letter to the church in Rome?"

"Sure. Memorized a lot of it."

"Do you remember anything being tied up?"

I stared at him, searching my memory.

Linus began chuckling, and then laughing. "I think I know the answer," he finally said, wiping his eyes. "Let me guess."

"Please do," said Job, a big smile on his face.

"The whole creation."

"Exactly!" shouted Job. I looked at him, completely blank.

"And it could not be loosed until the sons of God -- us, not the

Watchers! -- came. Right?"

"Exactly," said Job again. "Well done." Turning to me, he said, "Can you quote it for us now?"

"Something about 'the creation itself will be set free from its bondage…'?"

"'…and obtain the freedom of the glory of the children of God'. Yes."

He looked around at us, as serious as I had ever seen him.

"And as far as Orion, that could not happen until we came, and until we resolved the situation with the Dominant being kept here. The cords of Orion, my friends, have been loosed. Thanks to you!"

Twenty-Five

As the evening grew late, a slender bearded man came from the kitchen and stood behind Job's chair.

"Ah, there you are. Some wine for everyone, if you please?"

The stranger bowed, and disappeared into the kitchen.

"Job?" I asked, "Who is that?"

"An old friend. I'm surprised you don't recognize him!"

I looked at the others, and they shook their heads.

The dark-skinned stranger returned with goblets of wine for everyone. He met our eyes, as he brought the tray around to each person, but said nothing. I had no idea who he was.

As Job took his glass from the tray, the man bowed.

"Thank you, 'Athaq," said Job. "That will be all."

The End